Praise for PsycheDeliah

The dark novel succeeds on several levels... the protagonist, Paul is believable as a desperate man eager to rekindle his marriage to a gorgeous woman who is clearly out of his league. He is a character who becomes increasingly self-aware as the story progresses, discovering more and more about himself as a man, a former husband, and a sexual being in ways he'd never imagined. A gripping, titillating amalgam of provocative, interpersonal melodrama and effective noir thriller.

Kirkus Reviews

A spirited mélange of neo-noir detective storytelling, southern California satire, outraged screed, and vigorous erotica, Jensen's provocative thriller finds hero/naif Paul (a "vanilla boy of supreme proportions") plunging into the world of underground sex clubs and rich-dude fantasies on a quest to find and maybe avenge his errant wife, Deliah... This snappy, explicit erotic thriller builds to a psychedelic conspiracy to take down predatorial men.

BookLife

PSYCHEDELIAH

A Novel

KITE JENSON

FURTHEST PRESS

Copyright © 2021 by Furthest Press

Furthest Press, 29138 Pacific Coast Hwy., #330, Malibu, CA 90265.
ASIN: B09GKZLHKV
ISBN: 978-0-9651190-7-8
Ebook ISBN: 978-0-9651190-8-5

ONE

If Only

ON OUR LAST NIGHT TOGETHER, I took Deliah gently. I ran my hands through her hair, nibbled her ear, trailed kisses down her belly, and told her she was beautiful. I even flicked my tongue across her clit for the better part of an hour—softly and slowly like all the books advised.

She moaned and wriggled, but she didn't come. I whispered that she was my soulmate, my queen I'd cherish forever. "I love you so much," I cooed. Seeing her in our bed, sprawled out naked in the candlelight, I felt a shiver of amazement that she was mine. My incredible goddess wife.

It was the same shiver I felt every time I saw her sweet face framed by her long blonde braids and her delicious chestnut skin, her tight little ass, her perky breasts that were just the right size. She was the whole package—the image of perfection I'd always fantasized about as a boy.

I stroked her thighs as my tongue delved deeper. My hands began to play with her nipples. "Tell me what you want," I said. "I'll do anything."

She raised her head slowly and gave me that look of sadness I'd seen a hundred times before. Then she put her head back down on the pillow and closed her eyes. I knew exactly what that meant—or so I thought. Funny how the little cues that you're sure you understand are actually the most elusive. For six years, I'd responded in the same manner and she'd never once indicated discontent.

My cock was hard. Not super hard, but hard enough to get the job done. I abandoned my licking, just like I thought she wanted, and I climbed on top of her. I was very careful, as usual. I kissed her softly, stroking the back of her neck, grazing the tip of my phallus against her wet clit. And then I entered.

Like I said, I took her gently. Our souls intermingled in the darkness, with me doing all the work, in and out, tenderly and exquisitely. Because I loved her so much.

I thought it felt good for her too. I thought we were connecting more deeply than usual. That's what I wanted to believe anyway.

How utterly full of crap I was. I'd lived on the earth for 29 years and still I was a boy. I didn't know a god damn thing about reality. All my accumulated knowledge had been distorted and manipulated, baked in the oven of delusion.

I was the sucker. This world we lived in was a jungle. A predatory jungle of greed and deceit, manipulation and abuse.

Everything around us made that crystal clear, yet I refused to see it—even though I'd been a victim of it as early as age eight. I blocked out my own experience, my own direct knowledge, and convinced myself I inhabited a loving society. A society based on respect and compassion and fairness. What an idiot.

I hadn't been paying attention to what underlaid the MetLife billboards, the Nike commercials, the Google Ads that surrounded us. I focused on the shiny veneer of our capitalist system, not the hideous injustice upon which it was built. And every day, I dedicated myself to the mantra of sharing and intimacy. That was what would make our marriage last—all the therapists said so.

For the six years we were together, I only looked at Deliah. It's true. My eyes never stole a glance at an unsuspecting female's breasts. I always turned the other way, even if a hot babe was bent over on a beach volleyball court, showing me her bikini-clad ass. When the guys at work went to the local strip club, I stayed at my computer and worked on graphics files. I didn't even think dirty thoughts. Who needed that nonsense? I was completely devoted to my wife.

So it was on our last night together. The perfect husband, I made love to her like she was a rare and delicate orchid. Striving to bring us to new heights, I remained inside her for as long as I could, imagining by some miracle she'd orgasm with me.

Deliah almost never came though. I'd taken her over the edge a grand total of three times. Those three times all occurred in our first year of marriage and only after we'd consumed copious quantities of Merlot.

Still, I followed my formula to the tee. I pumped her a little harder, but not too hard. I grinded her once more with a bit more force. Then I emitted a barely audible groan, pulled out with surgical precision, and came on the pre-approved region of her belly.

We held each other in an effete embrace for a minute or so, neither of us acknowledging her lack of release. I caressed her back for a few seconds, in a feeble attempt to deny the banality of our union. We both sighed and Deliah retreated to her side of the bed.

The entire routine was a catastrophic error, a cosmic debacle, a singular proof of my non-existence. I didn't yet know it, of course, but all my techniques had been one hundred percent wrong. My performance, from beginning to end, was the *exact* inverse of what she sought.

What I should have done was grabbed her by the wrists and tied her to the bedpost. I should have propped her up on all fours and demanded that she hold her ass high up in the air for me. "Give it to me!" I should have howled.

At which point, I should have spanked her hard, right on those smooth brown cheeks. I should have taken out a leather whip and marked her so that her ass throbbed and stung and quivered. I should have pressed the handle of the whip against her hard clit, making her buck and groan. I should have tugged her cute little pussy lips, stretched them, and spit on them too.

When she whined and whimpered, I should have slapped her tits, her clit, maybe even her face, and pulled her hair. "You know you want it!" I should have insisted. "Beg for more, slut!"

If she didn't whimper in exactly the tone I wanted, I should have smacked her harder and pinched her nipples. "You want to be used, don't you? Tell me you want to be used! Come on, say it!"

And when she finally admitted it, when she finally gasped, "Yes, please," I should have withdrawn any further attention and affected my most stern voice. "Say all of it, slut!" I should have boomed. "Say it properly or you'll get nothing more!"

Her pussy would have been soaking wet then. It would have been so wet, she would have felt her juices dripping down her thighs. Her nipples would have been so rock hard, she would have had to finally release the truth. "Yes, I want to be used!" she would have cried. "Please give it to me! Pleeeeeeeeeeeeeeeease use me, Paul!"

And then I should have gotten behind her and slammed my hard cock deep into her pussy all the way to the hilt. Very hard. Again and again and again.

If only I'd taken her like that, she still would have been alive today.

TWO

A Classic Dick

To BE FAIR, it wasn't quite that simple. I wouldn't have been able to take Deliah that way even if I'd known the stakes. At least not then. For one thing, I was a vanilla boy of supreme proportions. And secondarily, there was the matter of my childhood trauma, which had been quietly hollowing me out my whole life.

But everything seemed perfectly normal the next morning. As we ate our favorite breakfast of eggs and bagels, Deliah caught me up on her auditions for the day. I promised to have a good movie cued up for us that night and she gave me a parting kiss on the lips. Her backward glance as she headed out the door was the last time I ever saw her beautiful face.

My day at the office passed without significant incident. Time droned on at the normal rate, offering no indication of what awaited, and my colleagues at MediaCow largely kept to themselves. I ate a sandwich at my desk, breaking from my workload only to download *Crazy Rich*

Asians for the evening's festivities since Deliah loved rom-coms.

Not until I returned home did fate call. The instant I opened the front door, there it was, wailing like a siren: A lilac-colored Post It Note affixed to the kitchen counter. I sensed its gravity by the color alone, but that didn't stop me from rushing over to read its message:

I'm sorry, Paul. This will be better for both of us. Just know that I never really loved anybody. Love, Deliah

The first question crashing through my mind was what the hell did she mean by 'this?' *What* will be better for both of us? I barely noticed the intrinsic inconsistency—that she could say she never loved anybody, but then sign the message "Love, Deliah." Classic god damn motherfucking life.

As the blood vessels in my head expanded, the world turned to slow motion. Thump, thump, thump. The rest of my insides contracted like an accordion. What I'd always suspected would happen, but feared too much to face, had finally arrived: our divorce. 'This' was our divorce. Thump, thump, thump.

Why did I abhor the idea of separation when our union had given us so little happiness? How could I have loved her so much when she'd never loved anyone at all? What collision of sheer madness caused us to share the same living quarters for six years?

Lifting my throbbing head to survey our condo, I realized almost everything of value was gone. The paintings, the leather couches, the wall units, the flatscreen TV, even our four-poster bed. I felt an odd sense of relief to be rid of the evidence of our sad materialism, but it hardly compensated for my thumping fear. What now? Why? How?

I almost laughed when my eyes landed on the one remaining piece of art, a small sculpture of the goddess Kali, leftover from the days when we'd experimented with Tantric yoga. I could only assume it was left intentionally —Deliah viewed the eastern religions with extreme intrigue and utter disdain. We both had been led to believe by various new-age healers that Tantra could help revitalize our sexuality, but no such luck. It was all bullshit, as usual.

So now I had a two-bedroom condo in Marina del Rey with nobody to share it with but a goddess of destruction. It was fucking perfect. Divine. Accurate. Spiritual. This is what it meant to live in the jungle and cut your deals in West Los Angeles. To play by the rules and believe in hope and justice and the beautiful girl next door.

I picked up Kali and held her in my palm. As I contemplated whether to smash her against the fireplace or hurl her through the window, my iPhone rang. The device always managed to interrupt me at the worst possible time and this was no exception. I mock-smiled at the futility, then I put down Kali and grabbed the stupid thing.

"Hello?"

"Pauly, how's it going, brother?" It was Deliah's entertainment lawyer, a pinch-faced guy named Gene Maher.

"Uh, is Deliah there or what?"

"I know this is a very difficult time, Pauly," he continued. "She's not in the office, but she wanted me to apologize to you about all the stuff being gone."

"Wh...what?"

"You're a stand-up guy," said Maher. "I've always felt that way and I know Deliah does too."

"Let's dispense with the BS, Gene. Is there a reason for this call?"

"She really wants you to be happy, that's all. And I can tell you this with perfect honesty—she wants nothing but her fair share. In fact, she wants less than her fair share, Pauly."

"Okay..."

"You're not going to retain a lawyer, are you? I hope you're not considering that Pauly, because the last thing either of you needs is more pain."

"Right," I mumbled. "Pain is bad."

"Is it the four-poster bed? Is that what's bugging you? Deliah thought that might bother you and I think we can arrange a swap against something else if you want it back."

"Gene, please. Just send me whatever paperwork you need me to sign, okay? Divide our stuff however Deliah wants. I don't give a shit."

That night, I stayed up sketching on a pad of paper, playing with abstract shapes and forms. I found it soothing to return to basics. I hadn't put pencil to paper for years, not since I'd been an architecture student. Working for a gaming company in Santa Monica didn't exactly encourage one's artistic side—life in the fast lane hinged on being able to gleefully embrace every new trend, every technological advance.

I took the job at MediaCow because I couldn't get a single interview from a decent architecture firm. I'd been a top student at UCLA's School of Architecture and Urban Planning, but when I graduated the economy had bottomed out. No firm was hiring unless you were willing to take a job that paid practically nothing.

MediaCow, on the other hand, was flush with cash. They needed people who knew how to design environments as backdrops for their "eco-adventure" games. What they liked about me was that I actually understood how to render shadows. Evidently, not that many people could do it, especially for different times of the day. But when you study the subject enough, you start to realize how much shadow affects everything.

Originally, MediaCow hired me to fix their alpine forests. After I added all the shadow variations, they quickly saw how lame their underlying design was. If you've ever played one of MediaCow's old games, you know what I mean. Most of them have stylized mountains and meadows and lakes that don't look the slightest bit realistic. So when I added accurate shadows to their stupid landscapes, they looked even stupider.

That was when they enlisted me to flesh out all their environments. It turned into a never-ending process because as soon as I finished with one game, there was always another one that had to be put out before our competitors beat us to the punch. Day after day, all I did was toil on some glacier or cave or castle. I had a master's degree and here I was making glorified cartoons for teenagers. My friends from architecture school gave me endless grief.

But after a while, I stopped caring whether my structures got erected on the physical earth. If anything, I started thinking that the virtual world was actually more enduring. Real buildings had to deal with earthquakes and hurricanes and global warming—not to mention, the vicissitudes of politics in an age of decaying democracy.

The bottom line was that the job allowed me to support both of us while Deliah pursued her acting career. I liked being useful to her like that. She had a vision of reaching people to change the way they thought about life and she felt certain that acting was the way to achieve it.

To her credit, she'd managed to get a couple of bit parts in some major movies. But Hollywood wasn't easy, as we both knew. That's why I cut her extra slack when she came home from auditioning in less than thrilled moods.

Granted, I had no idea how my strategy would play out. No idea at all. I was just waiting for her to be happy so that we both could be happy. I figured it was simply a matter of time, like getting through graduate school or anything else.

Meanwhile, it seemed the prudent course to be courteous and make the best of things. I sent her a dozen roses on her birthday. I made her chicken soup when she was sick. And I told her I loved her every time I detected that sad look on her face.

But now, all that was left in our condo was crystal clear evidence that my strategy had been ineffectual, my love unworthy, my commitment insufficient. All that was left was crystal clear evidence that I was a dick.

A classic fucking dick.

THREE

This is Real

THE DIVORCE PAPERS arrived two days later. I kept looking for signs of Deliah amidst the legal verbiage, but I could barely locate her signature. How was I supposed to concern myself with the divvying of property when all I could think about was that I might never lie naked with her again?

The possibility of life without her thrust my hollowness to the forefront. Why weren't we negotiating over behaviors and duties instead of couches and computers? What did she need from me that I wasn't providing? And why hadn't she checked first to see if maybe I could provide it?

I yearned to tell her that it wasn't over yet, that we could still solve this riddle. If only I could talk to her, I felt sure I could persuade her. I would plead with her relentlessly. I would prostrate myself before her and beg for her to reconsider. This wasn't about pride and honor. It was our future. I'd gladly metamorphosize into whatever she wished if only I could be with her.

But Deliah left me no way to contact her and Maher

insisted he didn't know her whereabouts. I called her parents, who lived in Palo Alto, and they claimed not to know either. Same with her friends and acting buddies. I could only assume she'd gone out of town to clear her head.

According to the settlement agreement, Deliah was to get the Volvo, most of the household goods, and all of our savings. I was to keep the condo and my Jeep. My retirement fund was to be prorated between us.

I decided to sign the paperwork immediately, without quarrel or protest. It seemed feasible she might return at any minute. I wanted her to know that I respected her space, as well as her decision to file for divorce. Cooperating gave me an opportunity to demonstrate my love.

There was no question I was coming out on the short end, especially since we'd been forced to take out a second loan on the condo, tapping most of the equity. But she could have easily asked for spousal support. Besides, I still didn't see this as a real ending. At least my brain didn't consider it as such.

I spent the rest of the week buried in my work. The mundane activities of life made little sense, like eating food, watching television, or talking to other human beings. But the shadows still worked. They still followed the same laws and covered things up in the same way. Somehow I took comfort in that.

It seemed particularly appropriate that I was designing my first aquatic environment—a giant underwater city in the Atlantean tradition. The deeper I placed my structures in the sea, the more obscured the shadows got, although they never faded completely. I experimented with eliminating them on the bottom rung of coral reefs, but their absence took away the mystery and integrity of the place. That's a funny thing about shadows—the smaller and lighter and less visible they get, the more you miss them when they aren't included.

AFTER A FEW DAYS, my coworkers got word of my divorce. I never told any of them, but in a town where half the population is lawyers, news like that doesn't stay secret too long. It didn't help matters that both MediaCow and Maher's office were located on Wilshire Boulevard, only two blocks apart.

Everyone at work voiced the usual sympathies. I smiled politely, declining their Lakers tickets and dinner invitations. Our breakup had been a long time coming, I explained mechanically. We were both going to be happier now. That was just the way things went. All for the best. To new beginnings. This was L.A., after all.

The difficulty arose when Friday arrived. In spite of my protests, I was forced to accompany my coworkers for lunch at the Jet Strip. Watching naked girls shake their moneymakers would ease my mind, they assured me. I tried to put on a happy face, but it didn't work in the least. I preferred my wife's body above all others.

Steve must have noticed my reservations. A paunchy, balding guy, he worked in the accounting department and I'd barely traded five sentences with him in the past year. I guess he starting feeling guilty because about halfway through the second dance set, he asked me if I wanted to get some fresh air. Grateful for any excuse, I followed him outside.

"I don't know if this is right, Paul," he said. "Maybe I ought to keep my fat lip shut. But I've tossed it around nonstop since I heard about your divorce and what I've come to is this: I'd want to know if I were you. You know what I'm saying?"

"Not really," I said.

Steve let out a long sigh. "About two months ago, I went to one of those underground clubs with a friend of mine. Deliah was there. Dressed to kill."

"It must have been an acting gig or something," I speculated.

"I wish it was. She was in a bondage outfit, Paul. A guy was leading her around on a leash. It was a very weird scene, trust me."

"Sounds like they were filming. So what?"

"You don't understand. She was with this guy—romantically. He was fondling her ass and making her lick his belly as if she were some sort of pet."

I felt the hollowness expand further within me, like a vacuum cleaner sucking up a part of myself I didn't know existed. "What was the name of this place?" I asked.

He paused for a long moment, then sighed again. "People call it The CuntGrind. It's sort of a code name. I don't usually go for stuff like that. A friend visiting from out of town heard about it."

"Sure, I understand. I appreciate the information, Steve."

"You're not upset I told you?"

"No, of course not," I lied. "This is good. This is real."

FOUR

You Want One or Not?

THE FACT IS, I knew nothing and nothing knew me either. There was nothing to know because it was all unknowable. Anyone who says differently is a piece of shit liar.

The history of civilization tells us that power comes to those who take it. You don't need to know things. You just need to take them. Make the claim whether warranted or not. Just make the motherfucking claim. Or else be reduced to yet another victim. One more slave in chains. Led by a leash.

But what was worth taking? Was power really an acceptable substitute for knowledge? I couldn't say because the vacuum cleaner inside me refused to turn off. Scooped out like a pumpkin, I only wanted to be alone. I fiddled with a few graphics files at the office, then I retreated back home.

Maybe Steve had only seen someone who looked like Deliah at the CuntGrind. Or maybe he'd just gotten a little too toasted on margaritas. But that was foolish hope. In my gut, I had no doubt he'd hit the mark. If anything, whatever he projected onto the scene was far less than the true imputation.

That whole weekend, I sat on the floor and stared at the walls. Minute by minute, hour by hour, I predicted where each muted shadow on the curtain would fall. It was all very educational—I generated a whole slew of new ideas for the Atlantean waterscape. And then I resolved that I was never going to do another day's work at MediaCow.

On Monday, I slept in and phoned my boss from home. It was already 11:00 am and he started yelling about deadlines. I calmly informed him that I couldn't help him out anymore. When he realized I was quitting, he offered to raise my salary by fifty grand, but I barely paused to consider it.

"I can't work anymore," I explained.

"Look," he replied, "I'll give you a few weeks to sort things out, but I personally think you'd be better off staying here. A woman isn't worth screwing up your life over. You're a good guy, Paul. There's nothing you can do but move on."

"I intend to move on. That's why I'm quitting."

"It's your call. But if you walk away now, this job isn't going to be waiting for you."

"Understood. Completely."

For the rest of the day, my mind scrolled through the various activities I could perform, but none of them seemed the slightest bit relevant. Emptiness pervaded. I curled into a ball on the living room floor and found myself recalling my parents' divorce when I was five years old.

Like my own divorce, theirs came swiftly without advance warning. In my parent's case, however, the three children were divvied up just like their material possessions. It was a lesson in soul-trafficking from which I never recovered.

One sunny California morning, I awoke to the sound of the garage door opening. I heard voices, a trunk slamming, car doors closing, more voices. When I went to look out the living room window, I saw the family station wagon backing down the driveway.

My mother was at the wheel. My brother and sister, both older than me, sat in the bench seat behind her. Boxes and suitcases filled the rear of the vehicle.

The station wagon was moving slowly and I desperately wanted to run after it, but the horror of the spectacle made me feel like I was covered from head to toe in molasses—as if I were in one of those dreams where I couldn't move at all. By the time I regained control of my body, the vehicle was nowhere to be seen.

"Where'd they go?" I cried out to my father. "Why'd they leave without me?"

"Son," he replied stiffly, "we all sat down last night and agreed your brother and sister will be living with your mother from now on. Buck up, you'll get used to it."

I wondered why I didn't qualify to be part of the sit-down, as I never would have agreed to such a decision if I'd been given a vote—my siblings were like gods to me. But even at age five, I knew better than to ask.

It was the first of countless invalidations, countless proofs that I was invisible, that I did not exist. My wants and needs did not matter. To anyone. The message was delivered powerfully and forcefully, day after day, year after year, by my college professor father. Yet somehow I never seemed able to face the facts.

For the next eleven years, my mother took me out to dinner once a month. These outings were the sum total of my interactions with her—two hours a month, usually at Marie Callender's. Maybe that's why I became so good at math, although the calculations weren't particularly difficult. After age five, I received a grand total of two hundred and sixty-four hours of mothering. What most kids got in a month or two, I got spread out over eleven years.

Not that I'm complaining, though. Those two hundred and sixty-four hours actually saved my life. Because even though my mother wasn't exactly equipped to be maternal—she'd been repeatedly raped by a family "friend" for much of her childhood—she did listen to me to the best of her ability. It would be an exaggeration to say that my father listened to me for even two hundred and sixty-four *seconds* during those eleven years.

To get through the ceaseless neglect, while my professor father preyed on doe-eyed college girls, I developed the habit of staring out the window and watching cars pass by our house. I made a game of guessing how many cars would pass before it would be his. When I got tired of being wrong, I would raise the stakes. I would tell myself that if his car was not one of the next ten cars, then it would mean I would die. I occupied myself for hours like that.

I never told anyone about my unusual pastime, not even Deliah. When we decided to move in together, she made a big deal out of finding a condo that had no views of any roads. She only wanted to see plants, pools, or other buildings. It took us a while, but we finally found one that met the requirement. I'd always thought she was very clever to care about such things, but now I wasn't so sure. For the first time since moving there, I regretted not being able to see cars.

I decided I had to get some air. The Atlantean project was still on my mind, even though I no longer had a job, and I felt an urge to be somewhere tropical. In graduate school, I used to frequent a Polynesian restaurant on Pico Boulevard, so I figured I'd check out old haunts.

When I got there, I noticed the name had been changed. The exterior of the building still featured tiki sculptures and South Pacific murals on the walls, but the doorman informed me that the establishment was under new management. In addition to a full dinner menu, they now offered live dancers on two stages. "It's all very tasteful," he assured me. I shrugged and went inside.

The hostess seated me at a booth with a direct view of the main stage. I studied the menu for a long time, barely paying attention to the dancers. A smile almost came to my lips as I imagined how Deliah would react to seeing me there alone.

She always thought it was weird that I didn't like to look at other sexy females. When I shared my concern about objectification, she said I was just hiding out because everybody was an object, like or not. Fuck it, I thought. If this is what captivates the human species, so be it.

Three women were dancing to "Born to Be Wild." They slithered amongst each other, gyrating and teasing, removing their blouses and skirts until they had on nothing but bikinis. Men cried out for them to take it all off, but the girls were oblivious. They'd done this routine a thousand times. No one would interrupt their process. Even their eye contact was a sham, an ego-booster constructed solely to solicit further revenue.

After I ate my dinner, one of the girls approached me. "How 'bout a private dance?"

I shook my head.

"There'll be lots of touching," she said with feigned innocence.

"Maybe you can help me," I replied.

"I'd love to..."

"Have you heard of a place called The CuntGrind?"

"Are you talking dirty to me?" she cooed.

"It's an underground club."

Her eyes turned cold. "Honey, I'm just doing dances. You want one or not?"

I slipped her two twenties. "Have you heard of it?"

"Talk to that guy over there." She pointed to a long-haired disc jockey in a sound booth. Then she snatched the money and stormed off.

FIVE

Rootless, Shiftless, Hopeless

REEKING OF POT, the DJ waved off my bribe and treated me like a long-lost friend. He explained that every Thursday night The CuntGrind set up shop at a different location. New invites had to pass a test, as some earlier gatherings had ended up in arrests for lewd conduct. He rattled off a telephone number without my even asking.

I called it a few minutes after leaving the restaurant and the woman who picked up launched into a barrage of questions. How old was I? How much did I weigh? How tall was I? What was my occupation? Did I have any arrests? Was I Dom or sub? I stumbled at the last question, but managed to blurt out "Dom."

The woman seemed satisfied enough. She told me to go to a bar in Hollywood called Ceci's and ask for Vic. "Be there between 10 and 11 tonight or whip your own ass."

At exactly 10:30 pm, I entered the seedy hole on La Brea. It was packed with mostly a leather crowd. Before I said a word, the bartender directed me to a young couple sitting in a booth. They looked like brother and sister, both barely over 18, with peach-fuzz smooth faces and Deadhead attire.

As I approached the booth, they jointly said, "CG?"

"Yeah," I replied.

"He's not bullshit," said the girl, staring at me intently.

"No, doesn't look like it," agreed the boy.

She stared a moment longer, then flicked me a business card. It hit my shoulder and dropped to the floor before I could catch it. They both laughed. I picked it up and saw it listed a Pep Boys automotive shop in Reseda. My brow furled.

"Turn it over, sweetheart," said the girl.

I did so and noticed a handwritten address.

"Midnight, Thursday," mouthed the boy.

THE NEXT MORNING I went to Maher's law office. He wasn't there, but the secretary said I could wait. I felt like total shit. The thumping in my head seemed continual and raw emotions kept churning through my nervous system, making it near impossible to focus on anything.

Finally, Maher showed up lugging a box of files and looking even worse than me. "Come on back," he said.

I followed him into a rear chamber where he checked his messages and sorted through a stack of papers. Then he turned to me with a thin smile. "That was real good of you not to contest. You're a mensch."

I nodded my head blankly.

"How're you holding up?" he asked.

His question caused the thumping within me to coalesce into a single taut lump in my throat. "I need to see her," I warbled. "Please, Gene. Tell me how to find her."

"I wish I could, I do, but I don't have any contact information. Zero. She was adamant about that."

"How could you have recorded the divorce without an address for her?"

Maher smiled again. "As usual, you impress me, Pauly. I have an address, yes, but it's just a mailbox in a UPS store. That's a perfectly legit address. I helped her get it myself because she was an absolute basket case about making sure you wouldn't find her."

"But why?" My eyes were watering now. "I love her. I would never hurt her. I would never cause her any pain. Never. I swear, I wouldn't. I swear."

"Jesus, take it easy. I don't know why she's done this. We never discussed any personal details." Maher paused, evidently to assess the liabilities of further conversation. "Look, to be perfectly honest, I think she's crazy. You're a good guy, Pauly. Out of the hundred and fifty-four divorce complaints I've filed since hanging my shingle, you're the only defendant who's ever emerged from the process with some dignity. You're the only one who didn't retaliate back at the spouse and you're also the only one who was polite to me throughout. Okay? So I don't know what the fuck Deliah is all about. My suggestion to you is to forget her. I had to learn the hard way too, but let me tell you, there are women out there who will treat you well, who will respect the love you give them, and who will return it tenfold. Do something real smart and forget about Deliah. Go find yourself one of those other kind of women."

When I left the office, the first thing I did was scan the bus benches on Wilshire to find the most offensive advertisement placed by a real estate agent. I dialed the number and explained the situation. I had to unload my condo as soon as possible. It was absolutely urgent. A family emergency. If it required a distress price, so be it, as long as I could close the deal in a week or less.

At first, the agent didn't think such a thing was possible. She explained that escrows were usually sixty or ninety days, and even cash deals often required at least thirty days. But I described the unique location of the property, plus all the design upgrades I'd made thanks to my architecture degree. I emphasized again that I would take any reasonable offer.

The agent came over about an hour later. She seemed particularly enamored with what I'd done in the kitchen— clerestory windows, three lightboxes, recessed appliances, bamboo countertops, blah blah blah. She also remarked on the custom lofts in the living room and den.

On Wednesday, I got my first offer. It was ten percent below market value, which was better than I'd expected, so I accepted without countering. The way I figured it, I'd still come out with almost 60k after both mortgages were paid off and the agent got her commission. That hardly balanced Deliah's take, but so the hell what? I wanted out.

Fortunately, the folks making the offer were ready to move in ASAP and they didn't need a loan. Tech retirees from Israel, they had a ton of Etherium, which they planned to cash out. The agent said that our transaction might be able to close in six days.

My idea was to buy an RV and travel around the country. Rootless, shiftless, hopeless, and without grounds for involvement in the ordinary sphere of life. It sounded just right to me. Maybe I'd stumble onto some meaning and maybe I wouldn't, but at least I'd have an endless supply of new shadows—and more passing cars than I could ever count.

SIX

Madagascar Man

I ALMOST DIDN'T GO to the CuntGrind Thursday night. After replaying Maher's little sermon in my head and poking at a microwaved lasagna, I decided I was too fucked up to make a decision. I retreated to the bedroom, where I'd set up my camping cot in lieu of a bed, and I settled into watching *Braveheart*.

The evening could have easily bled into yet another sunrise. Tendrils of orange lapping at the blue-green ocean. The promise of youth, innocence, freedom. And not a single wince of pain. How comfy it all would have been if only I'd slept through the night.

Instead, I awoke from a fitful dream shortly before midnight and my *raison d'être* came rushing back. It wasn't a question over which I had any control. Not even a little. Without thinking or turning on a light, I slid into a pair of ripped jeans and a black t-shirt. Then I bolted out of the condo.

A thirty-minute ride in the Jeep brought me to a grimy

industrial warehouse in Van Nuys. The location was off the beaten path and I didn't see any foot traffic, but when I went inside I knew I'd found the right party—if you could call it that.

The dimly lit warehouse occupied about ten thousand square feet. No attempt had been made to decorate the interior, other than the occasional placement of a few dirty couches or chairs. At the rear, a live band played sparsely and haltingly, somewhat like Mazzy Star, but even more melancholy and ethereal. There was no dance floor, no bar, just a ton of vaping.

About three hundred people filled the space. Roughly a third of them were stark naked, most sporting clean-shaven pubic hair. The others were in various states of dress or undress, except for a few normals with attire similar to my own. Most of the outfits seemed designed to shock, like a dreadlocked woman wearing only tights and six-inch C-clamps attached to her nipples or a drag queen with a pet snake wrapped around their cock.

There were the standard accouterments too. Men in leather harnesses or silk loincloths, women in rubber corsets or black spandex, trannies in sequined gowns or feather boas. They each sported the expected assortment of piercings, tattoos, whips, paddles, and chains.

But the props and clothing were of little interest—not to me or anyone else. The actions being performed were what captured everyone's attention. At each cluster of couches and chairs, some different atrocity occurred. The spanking of a pristine cheerleader's ass, the stretching of a redneck biker's testicles, the dripping of hot wax on a naked starlet's tits.

Curiously, the recipients expressed no discomfort. After each administration, they remained still, waiting to see if they would be rewarded with further punishment. When more than a few seconds elapsed, they often resorted to begging.

"May I have another, Sir?"

"Please, just one more, Mistress."

"Thank you, Master, I've been very, very bad."

The primary spectacle took place in the center of the room, where three couches were connected to form a line. On the couches knelt a dozen subs, all in a row, each one presenting a bare ass to the onlookers. In front of them, a portly bearded man stood flogging the ass at the end of the line-up. With enormous cat o'nine tails, he bore down on it repeatedly.

The bearded man was clearly a regular. He said nothing and expressed no emotion. Nor did he make any effort to entertain the crowd or embellish his movements. Each blow was delivered slightly harder than the prior one, with perfect regularity, until at last the pummeled sub slid off the edge of the couch and crawled away. The next one then moved down the line for the flogging, while another volunteer mounted the couch at the other end.

I watched the procedure for almost an hour. On two separate occasions, I thought I saw Deliah enter into the queue, but I was mistaken both times. The jumble of flesh and leather and moaning interfered with my mental faculties. I found myself becoming increasingly confused by bodies that ordinarily I would have known did not match hers.

Finally, the bearded man relinquished his position to one

of his peers. He wound his way through the warehouse, clapping the backs of various big-bellied associates, as he headed for the bathroom. I followed after him, waiting by the sinks while he relieved himself at a urinal.

"Excuse me," I said, once he finished. "I'm wondering if maybe you can help me out?"

"Doubtful," said the man.

"I'm trying to find my wife. I thought maybe you might have seen her here." I showed him a photo of Deliah from my wallet.

"Uh-huh," he grunted. "Seen the bitch a couple times."

"You have? You're sure?"

"What I said, didn't I?"

"Do you know where she..."

The man took a hold of my shoulder. "The bitch is Laster's property now. She don't come here no more."

"What? I don't understand."

"You don't mess with someone else's property, boy. That's fundamental." The man stared at me with clouded eyes, then released his hold and walked back to his post.

His words penetrated to my core and the vacuum cleaner within me roared in a new way. I didn't fully comprehend what he meant, but for the first time, I questioned whether I really wanted to find Deliah.

Like the city of Atlantis, the CuntGrind straddled both fantasy and reality, truth and falsity, freedom and slavery. But one thing it made indisputably clear: Power wasn't just an acceptable substitute for knowledge. It was god damn fucking superior.

I had issues with all of it. I understood none of it. And the only thing I could think to do was to make a beeline for the exit. Before I could though, I was intercepted by a tiny female wearing a short black skirt and a pink bra with exposed nipples.

"I saw you watching me back there," she said, nodding at the whipping line. "You kept staring at me like you wanted something."

"I... I... don't think..."

"Will you smack my cunt?"

"I... I... I can't."

She rolled her eyes and turned to look for someone else when suddenly I regained my voice. "Wait, do you know where Laster is?"

"John Laster?" She started to giggle. "He's out of your league, Madagascar Man. I just want you to smack my cunt." She raised her tiny skirt and spread her pussy for me so that I could see her pink wetness and her hardened clit. "Smack it!" she commanded.

For a crazed moment, I seriously considered her proposition, but then the throbbing overtook me in a way that I couldn't override and my legs mechanically carried me back to the Jeep.

SEVEN

Like a River

I'D ALWAYS ENVISIONED the Internet as an enormous glass mirror sitting in a remote corner of the universe. It reflected everything in existence, yet contained nothing. It lied outside of time, yet always lagged.

The notion of the Internet as a global village? That was just a joke. Humans had no community. They'd never had any community.

The word 'village' sounded so romantic as if it offered a wellspring of compassion and support for its inhabitants, but villages had always been about one thing alone—survival. Humans might yearn for community, but they'd never find it. What they'd find was a bunch of individual sacks of greed.

That was why I turned on my laptop as soon as I got home. Circumstances like these were exactly what the web was made to address. I wanted the backdoor entrance to John Laster's disgusting life, with all of its myriad distortions. Because when you reflected a distortion, there was the remote chance you might stumble on a sliver of the truth.

People often complained they couldn't find what they were looking for online. They expected more than just a mirror as if somehow this Internet thing could make sense of the madness of its creators. I, on the other hand, was extremely satisfied with what I dredged up.

At work, I even developed a bit of a reputation as a cyber sleuth. When people needed an answer to some obscure question, they came to me. I could almost always discern the shadow beneath the reflection.

For this particular occasion, the first thing I did was visit the directory sites. Only two John Lasters were listed in California—one in Oceanside and the other in Pacoima. I doubted either was the Laster I sought, but I jotted down the numbers just in case.

Next, I checked the sites that tracked real estate holdings. That was a bit more interesting because they yielded four Californian addresses. Three were in L.A. county.

As I expected, the real payoff came from searching the blog sites. When I input 'John Laster Los Angeles,' a hundred and seventeen documents were returned. A hundred and fifteen of them were irrelevant, as they contained no real intel. But two of them reflected my target, one through the channel of money, the other through that of sex.

Neither one was written by Laster, of course. I knew he wouldn't be that visible. The first blog was posted by some dork in Pennsylvania who promised yet another get-rich-quick scheme.

"If any of you've had the opportunity to see John Laster's mansion, then you know the legend is true," he wrote. "The unbelievable accumulation afforded by dispensaries is a reality for those who can follow the discipline and rigor it demands. It's not just a small reality. It's a BIG reality!"

The second blog was from a site called Sabrina's Swinging Slut Shack. It occupied a section where Sabrina reviewed local swingers' parties.

"You'll probably never get an invitation to this top-secret event because even I didn't," quipped Sabrina, "but I have it from reliable sources that the hottest party of the month took place on the beach south of Neptune's Net. Hosted by the mysterious John Laster, the carnal extravaganza lasted two full days and nights. Thank Aphrodite that they didn't have to ride back home on horseback."

The findings far exceeded my expectations. I now knew two critical things about my target: One, Laster was a first-class asshole who owned multiple cannabis dispensaries. And two, he resided in a place that boasted the greatest ratio of first-class assholes on the planet—Malibu, California.

For a brief moment, I considered the possibility that Deliah had been snatched by Laster against her will. Maybe I could rescue her and she would be so grateful that her wounded soul would forever heal. Maybe she would not only settle for the marital bliss I offered, she would crave it.

But when I made an honest assessment of our six years together, I knew it couldn't be so. Her union with Laster was too perfect in its insanity. The terrible truth bubbled up from my throbbing heart like molten lava—Deliah's role as my wife had been yet another audition. There was no Deliah to get back.

My only consolation was that I now had a good idea of her location. If all went well, I'd be able to track her down and talk to her one last time—if only to tell her that I loved even her acting. Somehow that small purpose satisfied me enough to tuck myself into a sleeping bag and fall asleep on the cot.

WHEN I WOKE UP, I realized I'd overslept again. It was 10 am and I had a long list of chores to perform. The condo had to be readied, the Jeep traded for an RV, and I needed a post office box to receive my forwarded mail.

Fortunately, I didn't have much left in the way of possessions. I made an appointment for the Salvation Army to pick up the junk that remained. Then I headed to an RV dealership in El Monte.

The sales manager immediately tried to tempt me with one of those huge motor homes favored by rock bands, but I had no interest in luxury or enormity. Besides, my post-divorce net worth wouldn't permit either. Even with decent trade-in credit for my Jeep, I had rather limited options.

I settled on a used 21-foot Class B van called a Travato. It was younger than my Jeep by a year and it had everything I needed—a shower, a kitchen, a table, and a bed. Plus it came with a large water tank and an array of solar panels to make it self-sufficient. The fact that it sat on a Ram chassis called a "ProMaster" didn't dissuade me in the least.

The Travato drove almost like a regular van. I barely noticed the extra weight or the taller profile. On the way home, I stopped at my local post office, rented a box, and filled out the appropriate change-of-address forms.

When I got back to the condo, I called Deliah's friends one last time. None of them had any new information. I tried flattery, desperation, and guilt, but it seemed an inescapable conclusion that they really hadn't heard from her, particularly since they all were quite worried. I turned down four more dinner invitations and one hookup offer.

My follow-up call to Deliah's parents yielded a more discouraging response. "What the hell have you done?" shouted Walter, the father. "It's not like Deliah to miss her mother's birthday! I'm about one hair length away from calling the cops!"

"Actually," I replied, "I'd... I'd really appreciate that."

"Are you messing with me, Paul?"

"No, I'm serious. I've been wanting to file a missing person's report all week, but I didn't think it would look so good coming from her ex-husband. Maybe you could do it for me?"

Walter paused for a beat. "For Christ's sake, you still love her, don't you?" he said slowly.

"Yes... yes.... of course, I do."

"Come on up here, son. Come stay with us for a while. Get your affairs in order and come on up."

"Okay," I warbled. "Thank you, Walter. I will. Thank you so much."

I said goodbye and set down my phone. The moment I did, tears came gushing out like a river.

EIGHT

To a New Me

As to be expected, the escrow office screwed up my condo sale in about eighteen different ways. They pulled the wrong title report, incorrectly entered my social security number, forgot to contact the buyer's bank—all the usual antics. Par for the course in the digital age.

Fortunately, the errors only caused the transaction to be delayed by one day. I ended up needing the extra time to finalize my affairs, so the incompetence worked to my advantage. By Wednesday morning, I had the condo emptied and the Travato packed to go.

Locking the condo door behind me for the last time wasn't exactly easy. My new living quarters were tiny by comparison. I only had room for food, utensils, a few changes of clothing, some basic toiletries, a small stack of books, and a couple of mementos.

My biggest indulgence was wrapping the Kali in a spare blanket and wedging it into the corner of the rear storage cabinet. In spite of my mixed feelings about the sculpture, I wasn't ready to let it go yet. Somehow it gave me the courage to climb into the Travato and leave my past behind.

My first stop was the escrow office. To my amazement, the receptionist at the front desk had my check waiting for me. I traded it for the keys to the condo and she gave me a big smile. She looked like she would be a pretty good lay judging from the way she shimmied and giggled, but what did I know of such things?

I deposited the check at my bank, withdrew a few hundred bucks, and cruised up Lincoln Boulevard to the Pacific Coast Highway. As I approached Malibu, I kept thinking about the insanity of the PCH. Our sensitive shoreline was hardly the optimal place for sixty zillion cars and trucks.

The highway never should have been built there in the first place, especially not through Malibu. If our forefathers had a little more gray matter, they would have kept the land under the guardianship of the Chumash. Then all we'd see would be rows of planked canoes instead of a platoon of SUVs.

The family that acquired the original land grant for Malibu in 1891 knew a highway would spell disaster for their paradisical zone. The Rindge's fought the state of California for seventeen years before the madness of modern transit won. A carnage of asphalt between Santa Monica and Oxnard was laid in 1929.

But to hell with history. The current reality was that the city of Malibu straddled twenty-nine miles of coastline and comprised over forty-five thousand acres. Somewhere in the sprawling decadence of Spanish Colonial villas and post-modern mansions was a prick named John Laster.

Thankfully, the Malibu politicos were none too friendly to developers. They might have lacked the intelligence to spell their city's name—the true Chumash word was Humaliwo—but they understood enough to keep out the middle class. In other words, I only had to contend with a population of about 12,000 elites. I'd shaken hands with more than that many people at the last CES convention.

My first stop was Duke's restaurant. I ordered the fish tacos and proceeded to work the waitress. "I'm looking for an old college buddy of mine," I said. "He's supposedly a local here."

"Try the bartender," she replied.

The Laird-wannabe at the counter showed no look of recognition when I uttered Laster's name. Nor did he have any suggestions when I asked who else might know. I didn't blame him. Ignorance seemed a wise policy when it came to such matters.

After inhaling my tacos, I drove a few more miles to Surfrider beach and sat on the sand. About twenty surfers lounged in the water like seals. The waves were gutless, but it didn't stop the surfers from battling for dominance. An air of entitlement pervaded the location. I didn't fit, but my presence wasn't deemed too offensive, judging by the looks of the locals.

At the mouth of Malibu Creek stood a long-haired man with a purple-green longboard. His skin was so tan that it almost looked like ebony. He surveyed the incoming sets, adopting a Zen-like posture of indifference. Evidently, the waves were unworthy of his participation.

I approached him after he finished a conversation with

two sea-foamed females in wetsuits. "Hey, man," I said. "You seem like you've been around here a while."

"Couple of decades, I guess," he rasped.

"I'm looking for an old college buddy of mine who lives out here."

"Surfer?"

"Not sure."

"Well, there's two breeds here. The rich folk who do their Hollywood deals and drive beamers and the poor folk who wax their boards and drive pick-ups. I ain't seen a rich kook in the water since my buddy ran over Adam Sandler." He flashed me a long smile.

"I guess that probably means I'm in the wrong place," I said.

"It shows, bro."

I gestured goodbye and trudged back to the Travato. My mind felt fuzzy and feeble, so I rested on the bed and studied a Google map of the city. This wasn't supposed to be a difficult task. Maybe if Laster was a movie star or a politician I'd have a problem, but he was just a wealthy swinger. Big deal. A good journalist would probably be able to locate him in ten minutes.

I fired up the Travato and pulled out onto the PCH. Shops lined the highway on both sides. I queried clerks at liquor stores, gas stations, bars, and sushi restaurants. They all shook their heads and flashed me a look that said, "This is Malibu, dumbfuck. People live here because they want privacy."

Clearly, I was going about it in the wrong way. If someone pulled into Marina del Rey and started asking people where I lived, they'd never find me in a million years.

I knew maybe six people in the whole town. Even if Laster were more visible, the odds were still in his favor. This is America, for god's sake. No one knows anyone anymore. We're all anonymous celebrities basking in the glory of our eternal nothingness. And it feels damn good, thank you very much.

I spent the night parked on the shoulder of a pot-holed road on the "non-ocean" side of the PCH. A couple of old apartment buildings were carved into the hillside. It was one of the few places where residents who made less than seven figures could live. No ocean views, no Spanish tile roofs. I figured a modest RV would go unnoticed next to the pool cleaning trucks.

When I woke up, I schlepped down to the corner convenience store. Another pristine day with clear blue skies and balmy air. To celebrate my new freedom in paradise, I bought a papaya smoothie. Then I checked my phone and listened to a voicemail message from Maher.

"Paul," he said, "I've got some news for you. I shouldn't be telling you this, so don't you dare turn this against me, but I'm going to trust you on this one. Your wife—I mean, ex-wife—bought a new car and she wanted me to handle the registration and insurance. It's one of those hot-shit Mercedes convertibles, an AMG GT R roadster. Solarbeam Yellow. I'm telling you because I just got her plates and I thought you might be interested. They're vanities. I had to wait in line, charged her 450 clams an hour. What a joke. Anyway, are you ready? You're gonna love this. The license plate number is 2-A-N-E-W-M-E. Get it? To a new me. Can you believe that garbage? Now tell me you aren't glad to be on your own again!"

A Mercedes AMG GT R roadster. Give me a break. I'd seen one reviewed in *Motor Trend* the last time I was at the dentist's office. It was the ultimate mashup of ostentation, viciousness, and absurdity. Evidently, the Mercedes engineers didn't think it was enough to make a turbocharged engine with 577 horses and 516 pound-feet of torque. They had to *handcraft* the heinous thing too. A personalized internal combustion engine—just what the world needed, in the age of global warming.

I envisioned Deliah's mane of blonde hair flying behind her as she raced around a corner on Mulholland Drive. If she were with Laster, she'd probably be wearing a tight leather vest over a crotchless catsuit. Maybe he'd be feeling her tits as she drove. Who knew what other devices he'd be using to stimulate her at the same time?

Imagining the scene made me hate the car even more. Especially its color of Solarbeam Yellow, radiating in screaming opposition to the underground world of secrecy she'd entered. There was no shadow in Solarbeam Yellow—Deliah carried all of the shadow herself.

I climbed into the cab of the Travato and fired up the engine without bothering to tidy the kitchen or make the bed. None of it mattered. Some dishes spilled onto the floor as I pulled a violent u-turn to get back to the highway.

Just press the accelerator, I told myself. Just drive. Drive and drive and drive. Don't stop until you run out of fuel. Drive every remote road in the Santa Monica mountains, if necessary.

The pursuit shifted to pure instinct. That was all I had left in me. My brain wanted no part of it, no more agonizing over the probabilities. Where would a man like Laster put his abode? Should I search the hillside homes or the beach-side ones? Would Deliah's car be on the street or in the drive-way? What if it were in a garage? And what would I do when I found her?

My solution was not to look, especially not for a Solar-beam Yellow roadster. My eyes grew swollen and glazed like a blowfish. Just keep moving. Up every side road. Down every canyon. Around every cul-de-sac. Feel the rhythm like a surfer rides the wave. The yellow will come to you. The yellow always comes.

I recalled a day back in high school when a friend offered to share a joint with me. I partook, assuming it was just cannabis, but in fact the weed was laced with PCP. The rest of the afternoon I spent driving my Honda Civic in circles. My childhood trauma melted—at least temporarily—and the simple act of negotiating the vehicle around a corner felt like I'd attained nirvana.

The more I drove the Travato in my glazed state, the more that feeling came back. The streets blended together. The stop signs no longer impeded me. Traffic became my companion and the asymmetrical maze of the Malibu neigh-borhoods a source of comfort. I didn't need to find anything. I just needed to breathe.

Gradually, I traversed the eastern half of Malibu, where most of the homes were. Big Rock, Las Flores, Carbon Canyon, the Colony, Civic Center Way, Corral Canyon, even Latigo. The sun arced halfway across the sky and still I continued driving. For all I knew, I'd driven past Laster's home hours ago.

I veered off the PCH toward Point Dume, beckoned by the honeysuckle, wisteria, anise, and bougainvillea. Each vista grew more spectacular, as I wound my way to the Point. When I reached Dume Cove, I renounced it all.

Sheer cliffs overlooked a pristine sandy beach with crystal clear, blue water. I was less than an hour from the skyscrapers of Marina del Rey, yet I might as well have been on an island in the South Pacific. A lost man unto himself.

The setting sun imparted the rugged coastline with a virgin quality as if I were the first to discover it. Transfixed by the splendor, I pulled to the side of the road. The lump in my throat became a golf ball, as only one other beauty could compare.

And then my eye caught the reflection of a final ray of sunlight. I followed the glint down the cliffside street and there it was parked all by itself in front of a perfectly mani-cured estate—the Solarbeam Yellow AMG GT R with license plate proudly announcing: 2ANEWME.

NINE

Stick in Hole, Push

Even in the twilight, Laster's mansion showed favorably. Balancing complex surfaces and simple geometries, his home followed the best tradition of Mediterranean villas. Terra-cotta tile with oozy mud capped the imposing edifice, cylindrical towers rose above mottled adobe walls, and a courtyard with three patios and four balconies joined the rambling layout into one organic whole.

As I walked past a fruit-laden cherimoya tree, I struggled to hatch a plan. Why did I want to see Deliah? What did I want to tell her? How should I explain my presence?

My head offered no answers, just the throbbing ache that had consumed it for days. But my heart pushed me onward, yearning for one last connection, one last look into her eyes—even if winning her back was hopeless. That was as much of a goal as I could formulate.

I took a deep breath, stepped up to the front entrance, and rang the doorbell. A platinum blonde nymph opened the massive, wood-carved door. "May I help you?" she said. She struck me as too attractive to be a maid but too plainly dressed for anything else.

"I'm looking for Deliah Wolniak," I said.

"One second." She left the door cracked open and retreated. Before I could properly study the entryway, she returned and beckoned me inside. She led me to a sunken living room with an indoor koi pool and invited me to sit down on an enormous purple couch.

I waited there for quite some time. With each minute that passed, I became increasingly agitated. The bastard was obviously avoiding me. He had no right to deny me a visit to my ex-wife. He had no right to steal her from me in the first place.

Finally, Laster entered the room. He was a tall man with dark hair and a solid frame, but not quite as handsome as I'd expected. His tan skin and stylish beach clothing could not make up for a sallow complexion and disproportionate features.

"You must be Paul," he said, extending his hand. "I'm John Laster."

"Where's Deliah?" I said flatly.

He surveyed me up and down. "Deliah is gone."

"Gone where?"

"I really don't know," he replied.

"You're a fucking liar. That's her car parked out front, so cut the bullshit. I'm not here to take her away from you. I just want to talk to her, you dick. Show a little respect."

Laster smiled thinly. "How come you never talked to Deliah that way? I bet she would have liked it."

I leaped up from the couch and grabbed the collar of his cyan silk shirt. "Listen up, you stupid prick," I barked. "My marriage to Deliah was sacred. She's chosen to be with you now, so there's nothing I can do about that. But don't try to extend your sicko ways in my direction or I'll smack you down so hard you won't ever be able to wield a fucking whip again."

His gaze lowered as he regarded my hand on his shirt. "Point taken, Paul."

A couple of well-muscled men in suits approached the room. "You need us?" said one of them. I withdrew my hand tentatively.

"No worries," said Laster, gesturing for them to leave. "Not a problem."

"I think we do have a problem," I countered.

"Maybe. But it's not as big as I originally thought. You're nothing like I expected, Paul."

"And how does that matter?"

"You have a strong will," he said. "You understand little about the world, but you have a strong will and that's worth much more."

"And you're an arrogant fuck."

"That's exactly what I mean. I expected you would be ruled by fear, but I see no such thing. You're making me reevaluate the entire circumstance."

"Are you going to let me see Deliah or do we keep playing more games?"

Laster studied me with such stillness that for a moment I thought he was having some sort of seizure. "There are always more games," he said slowly. "But in this case, they yield no solution. I'll do whatever you wish."

"Then bring me Deliah."

"As I said before, Deliah is gone." He hesitated as he

stared at me again, then a softening overtook his face. "If you don't mind a walk on the beach, I'll escort you to her."

We exited out of the living room into a flower-filled courtyard with an undulating swimming pool. An elaborate masonry staircase led down to an arched gate. Laster punched in a security code and the gate swung open, revealing a moonlit canyon of sycamore trees and sage. At the mouth of the canyon, a few hundred feet away, I saw the reflections of soft waves lapping at the shore.

He guided us along a flagstone path to the sandy beach. It was too dark to fully appreciate the pure coast, but I spotted Big Dume about a half-mile away. Laster's home was positioned at the base of Little Dume, nestled in a serene and private bay. We rounded the point and headed east toward an equally unspoiled shoreline that I placed to be Paradise Cove.

The land around me looked as undeveloped as it had been five hundred years ago and I couldn't detect a single foul or synthetic smell. It seemed hard to believe that a thriving city of over fifteen million people existed less than twenty miles away. Money certainly could change one's reality.

After a few minutes, we came upon the first signs of human development—a small pier with an oceanfront restaurant. Laster picked up the pace as we continued down the shoreline. "We're almost there," he said. "Up ahead is Escondido Beach. Escondido means 'hidden.'"

I ignored his patronizing comment, having no interest in small talk. My only goal was to see Deliah. With each step, the thumping in my brain intensified and I feared Laster was somehow bluffing.

As the rugged cliffs gave way to softer slopes, I noticed a greater frequency of beachside homes. Sitting on enormous lots, most of the structures were neoclassical disasters. They looked more like hotels than houses. But then again, Hollywood was all about 'space' and Laster boasted that practically everyone who was anyone in the industry owned a home here.

Many of the properties included guesthouses carved into the hillsides below the obscene mansions. These tended to be comparatively modest, more coveted for their intimate ocean views than their architectural design. It was to one of these guesthouses—a faded wood bungalow comprising about a thousand square feet—that Laster pointed. "This is it," he said.

Obscured behind manzanita plants, the building could hardly be detected from the shoreline. My mouth became bone dry as Laster unfastened an iron latch that secured a weathered gate. He flashed me another of his still gazes, then we scrambled up a scraggly trail.

When we came to the bungalow's front door, Laster handed me a small silver key. "This is my gift to you, Paul Wolniak. Stick in hole, push."

"Huh?" I replied.

"Stick in hole, push," he repeated, nodding at the key.

I fitted the key into a rusty deadbolt and turned the knob to open the door. The interior was pitch black. "Deliah?" I called out. I flicked on a light and entered a small living room. Laster hung behind.

My head wasn't thumping anymore. Instead, a sharp pain replaced it, one that felt more like a knife piercing my skull. I hesitated a moment, then I walked down a narrow hallway leading to what I presumed to be the master bedroom. "Deliah?" I called out again.

The door to the bedroom was wide open, but when I first peered into the room, I could not see what I saw. I simply could not *see* it. It wasn't there. That wasn't what it was. It wasn't Deliah and I wasn't me. There were no boundaries. This wasn't life. This wasn't anything. No meaning existed. There was no light, no shadow, no earth, no universe. No existence.

And then I looked again. "Deliah!" I shouted. "Deliah!"

She lay on a kingsize bed, completely exposed, wearing nothing but black lace stockings and stiletto heels. Splayed out on her back, motionless, she was utterly vulnerable. Her wrists were handcuffed to the bedpost. Her legs were spread wide and raised up over her head by thick ropes that attached to her ankles from hooks in the ceiling. Every private part of her was visible.

"You're okay, Deliah!" I cried out. "I'm here now!"

Her eyes were wide open, but she made no response. I ran to her side, throwing my arms around her naked body. "My sweetheart, my goddess." I cradled her face and softly touched her cheeks, trying to awaken her. "Please talk to me, Deliah. Say something. Talk to me."

"She overdosed on Vicodin," announced Laster, as he entered the bedroom. "She's been dead since early this morning." He threw an empty prescription bottle on the bed. "I had no idea about her habit—I only gave her the psilocybin and a touch of mescaline. I hate painkillers."

I barely heard the words.

"Go ahead," he said. "Feel her pulse."

Somewhere deep within my piercing headache, I already

knew the truth—Deliah had courted this outcome. But all I could do in the moment was reach to feel her wrist. Her skin was cold and clammy, her muscles completely limp. I continued to grip her wrist for what must have been several minutes. There was no pulse whatsoever.

I still couldn't process it. Things like this happened in soap operas, movies, the nightly news. Not in my world. This was not my dead ex-wife lying in front of me, tied up in full bondage regalia, her body displaying all the trappings of deviance. This was not my Deliah with stretched and swollen nipples, raw labia and clitoris, whip marks across her thighs, belly, and breasts. No. It couldn't be. Impossible.

I released my hold of her and shifted my attention to Laster, who still hovered behind me. Suddenly, like a football linebacker, I lowered my head and ran straight for him, plowing into his chest with all my might.

"You bastard!" I screamed. "You fucking bastard!"

Laster careened to the floor, unprepared for the attack. He did nothing to resist my advance, nor did he right himself once I knocked him down. I continued to scream frenziedly between bursts of spitting on his face. "You killed her, you fucker! Look at her! My god! Look at what you've done!"

He didn't wipe the spit from his face, nor did he attempt to avoid my onslaught. Instead, he just let the saliva drip down his eyes and nose, staring at me with that same still gaze, waiting for me to finish my tirade.

"Jesus fucking Christ!" I yelled. "How could you leave her like that? It's despicable! It's inhuman!" I stripped off my shirt and gently covered Deliah's naked body. "Give me the keys to the handcuffs, you asshole! Untie the rope!"

"I don't think that's such a good idea," replied Laster quietly.

"Fuck you!" I screamed at the top of my lungs, my mouth foaming in fury. "Fuck you! You god damn motherfucker!"

"If you're going to report the incident to the police," he said, "it would be best to leave things as they are."

"And what the hell were you planning to do?"

"I hadn't decided yet. I was still considering the matter when you arrived."

"You're a fucking idiot if you think I'm not going to turn you in! You'll spend the rest of your life behind bars, you disgusting asshole! I'm going to see to it that you burn in hell!"

"You'll do what you need to do, just like Deliah did what she needed," he said softly. "If you make use of my gift, and if your will proves strong enough, perhaps what you need and what you want will become one and the same."

Then he turned and slowly walked out of the bungalow, without looking at me.

TEN

Long Gone

I'd always been a sucker for the twin concepts of duty and obligation. Everything I did was either because I figured I should do it or because someone else figured I should do it. Of course, the approach never got me anywhere—other than straight into a pit of despair.

I deluded myself into believing some reward would be forthcoming, eventually. You pay your dues, you play by the rules of the game, and one day everything suddenly makes sense. Life turns out to return a glorious dividend. Isn't that how modern society is supposed to work? Or is that just the law of stupidity and dumbfuckery?

Well, none of it mattered anymore. I was done with all pretense. If I ever had a captive audience, the first thing I would shout from the rooftops would be: "There is no civilization! Civilization is an illusion! An illusion spoon-fed to idiots, so the uncivilized can step all over them!"

There are no laws either. What a joke. Rules. Codes of conduct. Ethics. Morality. Give me a fucking a break. We're talking about a jungle—a jungle filled with a species of animal that is a zillion times more cruel and greedy and ruthless than the fiercest lion. Every time the news comes on, we get another piece of evidence of the brutality and corruption of our species. So why keep believing in a lie? Enter the jungle, my friends, where you already live, whether you like it or not.

Laster had murdered my wife, I knew that. Maybe Deliah had swallowed too many Vicodins, but even if she'd done so voluntarily, the bastard had facilitated it. He was responsible for her death. She never would have done something that stupid without his coercion or manipulation. Or his disgusting psilocybin.

When we were married, Deliah took two or three Vicodins per day, never more. She had a habit, yes, and I'd tried to get her to stop. But the acting world made her unbearably tense.

Sure, I knew there was a deeper issue lurking somewhere in her past—and I also knew to *never* raise the subject. That was our big, unnamed agreement. Silently and knowingly, we both promised to never, ever talk about our shit from childhood. Vicodin was the only thing that gave her relief.

She used painkillers throughout our marriage, practically every day, and yet somehow she craved *more* pain, not less. I couldn't give her what she needed, so she numbed her need. Her pain became the absence of pain, and she took painkillers to make the pain of the absence of pain less painful. Or did it make it more painful and was that the whole point?

Either way, it was a vicious circle. That was surely the

fault of Laster. I could see it all now. She was his perfect victim.

If she got more doped up on Vicodin, he could use her that much harder. She would be able to enjoy even more pain, more abuse, more whipping. How could she resist the temptation? Laster was playing with fire.

It was just like with money—once you tasted it, you kept going back for more. You worked harder, so you could spend more, so you could live less, so you could work harder, so you could die. The orgasm was a small death anyway, right? Everyone knew it hurt to cum, and everyone lived for the next chance to cum.

But that didn't give me the slightest peace of mind. Not even a tiny bit. It was one thing to fall prey to a system foisted upon us since birth and a whole other thing to succumb to a new system designed by a sick bastard.

I could accept capitalism and how it sucked our marrow clean, but never could I accept John Laster and his new version. That motherfucker took something that was not his right to take. End of discussion. End of analysis.

And that was why, as soon as Laster walked out of the bungalow, I resolved to follow my own code. I knew the authorities would be a total waste of time. Even if they bought my story, even if they determined that Laster was guilty, he would have the best attorneys, the best alibi, the best expert testimony. And even if a jury finally nailed Laster, the fucker would be coddled in the prison system. No way was that a good enough outcome for me.

There was only one solution. To kill the sick asshole myself. To look him straight in the eye, with the same god damn stare he'd given me, and pull the trigger. To lodge a bullet so deep into his cerebral cortex that all the pain he had caused others would finally be returned to his evil soul. And then to let the pain drip, drip, drip out of that terrible brain onto the dirt where it belonged. Until his sick being was forever empty and void and null.

That was the only way to vindicate Deliah. To right her wrong, to make all the prior pain recede once and for all, I had to replace her departure with an even bigger one. All the suffering, all the loss, all the tragedy would finally be released, evaporated, concluded.

But I wasn't going to be a fool about it. Even an uncivilized man had to follow certain procedures to win the game. This was my one chance to finally beat the system, to finally turn the tables in my favor.

So the first thing I did, once Laster was out of earshot, was to pull my phone out of my pocket and call 911. I told the dispatcher that my ex-wife was dead from an overdose, that it was a very disturbing scene, that they better send out the sheriffs, the coroner, the paramedics, the whole enchilada. And I punctuated my voice with all the right intonations.

I had no misguided notions about the efficacy of my actions. The only reason I called was to get the legal system off my back. And yes, sirree, you better believe I handled those officers with the ultimate of poise and aplomb. In other words, I told them everything they wanted to hear and nothing they didn't.

I laid all the groundwork while they took my statement outside the bungalow. "She'd been troubled even before the divorce," I explained. "Our sex life was why she left me. She wanted to explore the bondage scene and I didn't."

Lieutenant Carlson nodded his head like this was all perfectly ordinary. "So how did you find out she was here?"

"She'd been visiting a friend named John Laster," I said matter-of-factly. "He lives over in Point Dume. I dropped by his place this evening because I had some mail to give Deliah. He told me she was staying here. Evidently, Laster knows the owner and managed to convince him to let her use it. He gave me directions to the place and that's how I found her."

To my surprise, the cops didn't even drag me in as a suspect. Nor did they swing by Laster's mansion to question him. I suppose an overdose victim wearing only stockings and heels must have seemed pretty routine after all the bloody drive-bys. Unsolved murders were a dime a dozen in the murky shadows of Los Angeles.

Besides, my story was basically true. Laster would be able to run with it, even if he was only half as smart as he seemed. I didn't know how well he'd covered his ass at the bungalow, but whether or not he left semen or hair traces on Deliah's body wouldn't make much difference.

He'd be able to deflect suspicion for a while, no doubt. And by the time the lab samples came back, he'd be out of the picture. He'd be gone, yes, sirree.

Long gone.

ELEVEN

Thank You, You're Kind

By the time I made my way back to the Travato, it was early morning. The muted light seemed almost the same as when I'd first arrived at Point Dume. Dusk or dawn, what was the difference? Darkness didn't care whether it was diminishing or increasing.

I found myself imagining that I'd never entered Laster's mansion, that none of the insanity had ever happened, that time had somehow stood still—and that light now came from within each object, so that shadows could no longer be formed.

Climbing into the small quarters of the Travato forced me to reconcile. I was a small chunk of organic matter, floating chaotically amidst other chunks, with no connection to any other organic matter, nor to anything else. Whatever strategic role I once played on this earth had been yanked away forever. I was alone. I no longer even had an ex-wife.

The thought of sleeping at Point Dume made me nauseous. I gunned the ProMaster, peeled out of the dirt, and headed south. About thirty minutes down the PCH, I reached the Santa Monica Canyon and found a secluded neighborhood.

I tried sleeping for a couple of hours but had no luck, so I walked down to Patrick's Roadhouse to grab breakfast. As I sipped coffee, I considered my responsibilities. Should I inform people about Deliah? What about arranging a funeral, writing an obituary, filing a death certificate? Or, since I wasn't the spouse anymore, did these matters no longer concern me?

A call to Deliah's parents confirmed the latter. Being divorced, I had no legal say in anything. Both Walter and Iolana, Deliah's mother, had already been in contact with various authorities and didn't want my help. Iolana went a step further, blaming me for Deliah's death.

"How could you?" she sobbed into the speakerphone. "So selfish. If only you stayed by her... "

"For Christ's sake," interrupted Walter. "She's the one who divorced him. He couldn't be her knight in shining armor after she told him to get lost."

"I could have," I said. "And I should have. I should have known what Deliah was getting involved in. I should have protected her. There's no excuse."

Iolana burst into more sobbing.

"We still want you to come up here," said Walter.

"No, no, don't come!" cried Iolana. "You're not welcome!"

"The funeral is on Wednesday at Forest Lawn," said Walter matter-of-factly. "You'll be there, obviously, and you can come up the following day."

"It's not in Palo Alto?" I asked.

"No, Hollywood Hills. Yo-Yo and I decided that was the best place for her. It just made sense."

"I see. Okay. Hollywood Hills."

FOR THE NEXT FOUR DAYS, I installed myself in the Travato like a monk. All I did was sleep, meditate, and swallow a few dry crackers. I thought about making some calls to Deliah's friends, but each time I picked up the phone, I found myself incapable of swiping, clicking, or pushing anything on a screen. I couldn't even check my texts or voicemails.

My stupor soon extended to all my actions and thoughts. I became a sack of cells with no cohesive function. I couldn't feel anything, I couldn't do anything, I couldn't ponder anything, not even my plan to eliminate Laster.

It wasn't until Wednesday morning that a semblance of consciousness returned to my being. I had a reason to live again, albeit a pitiful one. With mechanistic single-mindedness, I put on the only suit I'd packed and guided the Travato into rush-hour traffic.

A snake of cars inched along Sunset Boulevard, then merged with an even bigger snake to ascend the 405 freeway. The drivers' faces were pure tension. Desperate to get where they didn't want to go, hating everyone with whom they shared the journey. We were arch enemies, every one of us on the road, and it was a perfectly level playing field. Adam Smith would have creamed his panties—all of it was guided by pure unadulterated self-interest.

I arrived at Forest Lawn ten minutes late. To my surprise, most of my coworkers from MediaCow were there.

So were Deliah's gang of wannabe actors, along with an assortment of friends, family, and relatives.

The priest spoke of the uncertainty of the human condition. He postulated that no single individual could ever hope to overcome such uncertainty. Not even in an ideal society of kindness and compassion. Only by embracing God could we rise above the vicissitudes of life and enjoy the unwavering love that is His gift to all.

He went on to explain that Deliah had passed away from a heart condition. This, he said, served as testimony to the warmth and sensitivity of her soul. "For sometimes, when the heart is strongest, it is also the least giving. But Deliah, we know, was one of the most giving humans any of us could have hoped to include in our lives."

Several more eulogies followed. I wasn't asked to provide one. None of the speakers seemed to know anything about the true circumstances of Deliah's death. That suited me perfectly well. I had no problem with the rest of the world believing that she died from "a freak side effect caused by prescription drugs," as one of the eulogizers suggested.

After the ceremony came the usual milling-about period. Each time someone conveyed their condolences, I nodded my head. "Thank you," I said. "You're kind." Most people actually believed I was listening to their words. I guess I sort of was. Iolana hugged me and babbled about how I was her only child now. My boss at MediaCow promised I'd get a corner office if I came back to work.

When the crowd thinned, I circled around the gravesite and climbed up to a grassy knoll. Deliah's friend, Cynthia, followed behind me at a respectful distance. She was from the acting crowd, the one who had come onto me a week earlier when I'd called her about Deliah's whereabouts. Somehow she looked different in a black dress, with her dark brown hair in a tight French braid.

"Hey, Paul," she said, "I know this is a difficult time, but I just wanted to say I'm sorry. Very, very sorry."

"Thank you," I replied. "You're kind."

"It was stupid—what I said before." She smiled nervously. "I'm not usually like that. I don't know what got into me. I'm really not that type of a person."

"Thank you. You're kind."

"I'd like to stay friends if you're willing."

I looked at her vacantly.

"Let me make it up to you," she continued. "I bet you could use a home-cooked dinner. I grill a really awesome halibut steak."

"Thank you," I said. We started walking toward the parking lot. "You're kind."

"We can do it any day you want."

"Halibut is good."

"Really?" She giggled softly, tugging on her braid. "So when should we do it?"

I motioned to the Travato. "I'll follow you."

TWELVE

Transference

———————

Cynthia had a little Craftsman bungalow in Silverlake. She invited me to read magazines on her couch while she put together the fixings for dinner. I did as she suggested, kicking off my shoes and perusing the latest fashion gossip. She didn't even ask me to light the barbecue grill.

I spoke less than three complete sentences over dinner, but Cynthia took it in stride. Between sipping Chardonnay and dining on halibut, she caught me up on her never-ending quest to get a spot on a popular daytime soap. She'd been called in four times already, most recently to meet the director. The way her nose wrinkled as she described the process made me think that Hollywood fame was not really what she wanted. As for most of us, the stated target functioned mainly by obfuscating the real one.

Maybe she sensed my skepticism. I didn't ask. I just politely cleaned my plate. After the tiramisu, she looked me straight in the eyes. "If you want to fuck me, Paul, that would be all right."

I heard her say it but could think of no reply. Instead, I studied the place where the fabric from her chair touched her back. The prospect of sex seemed absurd. If not to reproduce, why share genitalia with another person? What could possibly be more idiotic? Vast sums of money and countless hours were spent on the quest every day. And for what? It was so excruciatingly pointless I started to laugh.

"Shit, I'm sorry," interjected Cynthia. "I just did it again, didn't I?"

My head swirled in an unfamiliar way and I suddenly comprehended the obvious—there was no point to sex, there was no point to anything, and *that* was the point. I got up and slowly moved toward her. Out of my mouth came words, but I had no idea how or why I spoke them. "Maybe I should fuck you really hard," I said.

"God, yes," she replied excitedly. "As hard as you want."

Like a puppet, with no will of my own, I picked her up and carried her to the couch. Our lips pressed together and I laid her down on her back. As she pushed her tongue inside my mouth, my hands slid to her thighs, then reached under her skirt.

"Make me your slave," she whispered. "Please."

I pulled off her panties and gently teased her pussy. She moaned as I extended my touch to her hard clit. After flickering my finger across it with increasing intensity, she abruptly wriggled from underneath me and spun around onto all fours.

"Spank it!" she cried, pushing her ass high up into the air.

My hand reached to caress her smooth cheeks. I'd never spanked Deliah—or any other woman for that matter. It seemed like such a childish thing, something no grown woman would really want. But I couldn't see any harm as long as the recipient enjoyed it. Why hadn't Deliah ever asked me for it?

"Please!" squealed Cynthia. "I'll do whatever you say, as long as I can feel it!"

Tentatively, I removed her skirt, blouse, and bra. I had no idea what I was doing, but it didn't seem to matter. Somehow my hand began to spank her soft flesh.

"More!" she cried. "Make it throb!"

Her begging instilled a curious exhilaration. I struck her again, this time with increased force. Smack, smack, smack.

"Yes!" she groaned. "I love it! Harder!"

Each time I spanked her, she emitted more groans of pleasure. Her desire was infectious, uninhibited, addictive. I'd never considered my palm to be an erogenous zone, but feeling it strike her shapely ass was surprisingly erotic. I continued smacking her harder and with each sting of her flesh on my hand, I could not deny it—my cock grew likewise harder.

"More, more, more, more, more!" she squealed. Her frenzied need so overtook her being that it spilled into me, making me have the same want, the same need—to take her completely as my own. I raised my arm high over my head and prepared to bear down on her even harder.

"Don't stop!" demanded Cynthia. "Please! Teach me a lesson! I love it!"

It was lunacy, derangement. I actually wanted to hit her. I wanted to smack her with all my might to see how much pain her cute little ass could take. Where would she draw the line? How sore and red could I make it? When would she cease begging for more and instead plead for me to stop?

Suddenly, I thought of Laster. Loathing swept through me at the sight of her naked body posed so receptively to my advances. This was the same vulnerability he preyed on. Just as Deliah had been too weak to resist his sick mind, so too was Cynthia. Only now I was the ugly perpetrator.

Call it transference, projection, identity crisis—call it whatever the hell you want. I was carrying out the same evil cycle Laster had started when instead I should have been stamping it out and ending it forever. What the fuck was the matter with me? How screwed up could I be? It was more craziness than a single soul could stand.

"Please, Paul!" continued Cynthia. "Don't tease me! I have to have it! I have to!"

"No!" I screamed. "No more, Cynthia! You don't need anything! You don't need a god damn single thing!"

And I ran out of the house without stopping to retrieve my shoes.

THIRTEEN

Going Down

BACK IN THE TRAVATO, I struggled to calm myself. Yes, I'd lost focus. I'd made the age-old mistake of confusing my inner demons with the true external enemy. But a slip-up was to be expected. One could argue it was desirable. How could I fully extinguish Laster's fire unless I comprehended the extent of his flame?

Forget that I felt arousal. The important thing was to complete my task. I wanted a clean kill and I doubted my ability to undo Laster with my bare hands. Originality and courage meant nothing to me, so a gun was the obvious choice—preferably a handgun that required little skill or experience.

Cruising down Santa Monica Boulevard, I spotted a survivalist store with neon lights flashing "Open 24 Hours" and I pulled into the parking lot. My understanding of firearms was essentially nil. I didn't know what sort of laws governed their procurement, but I figured they must be rather lax. To my surprise, the clerk informed me that I would have to pass a thirty-question exam and wait eleven calendar days before I could purchase one of their guns.

Not a fucking chance. Not in Laster's sweetest dreams. I intended to kill the bastard that night. Obviously, there had to exist alternative channels through which to obtain the appropriate weaponry. This was L.A., after all. How hard could it be to find someone to sell me a gun?

I decided to return to the same part of Van Nuys where The CuntGrind operated. Evidence of drug activity was abundant there and I figured if a gang-banger could score me some crack, he could probably get me a weapon too. Besides, I liked the idea of buying Laster's death ticket in the same neighborhood where he'd violated Deliah's soul.

It took about fifteen minutes to locate the right street corner. A stocky kid with a shaved head appeared from out of the darkness when I adopted the requisite blank stare on my face. "'Sup?" he mumbled, opening his mouth wide. At first, I thought he was showing me his pierced tongue, but then I noticed a dozen or so tiny rocks nestled around his silver ball.

"Can you sell me a gun?" I asked quietly.

"Brah," he said with a confused look. "I ain't no shooter."

"I'll pay two fifty." I had no idea what the proper amount should be, but that seemed more than adequate.

The kid furrowed his brow, then pointed to a food truck a half-block away. "Roust Zeka."

"Zeka?"

"Tell her you're Billy's," he added. He pulled a phone out of his pocket and winked.

I guided the Travato into a narrow parking space and walked barefoot to the take-out window. After paying for an order of tacos al carbon, I inquired about Zeka. The cashier handed me a basket of food and motioned for me to sit down at an outdoor table.

Halfway into my second taco, I was approached by a muscular female with short purple hair. "I'm Billy's customer," I said, trying to hide my trembling hands.

"You got cash?" she asked with a sneer.

"Yeah."

"Five hundred."

"I told Billy two fifty."

She pulled a paper bag out of a large knapsack. "Two fifty each. This got two pieces in here. Comes with the stuff."

"Okay, but I only need one," I explained.

"And I only selling the set."

I nodded. "They work okay?"

"They ain't no toys, for sure."

I reached in my wallet and extracted five one hundred dollar bills. Zeka snatched them out of my hand before I had a chance to double count. After a long moment, she set the paper bag on the table. "Don't be hangin' round here no more," she warned.

"Thanks," I said, "I'm on my way." I picked up the merchandise, trashed the rest of my tacos, and headed for the Travato. When I got in the cab, my hands were still trembling so hard that I retreated out of Van Nuys without checking my purchase.

After reaching the safety of the Ventura Freeway, I mustered up the nerve to feel inside the bag. I wasn't particularly anxious to see the pistols—tools of death seem more suited to darkness anyway—but I did want to confirm that I had acquired more than a couple of lead weights.

Despite the fact that I was no firearms connoisseur, I had little difficulty verifying my success. There were definitely two handguns in the bag. With the tips of my fingers, I traced their hard metal handles, scalloped barrels, and crescent-shaped triggers. I even opened a small cardboard box and felt a row of smooth bullets.

Of course, I had no proof that the equipment would actually work, but the physics seemed fairly simple. You load a bullet in the chamber and pull the trigger. A firing pin strikes a plate that explodes the bullet and propels it out the barrel. What could go wrong? Maybe the guns would perform poorly, but I hardly cared about that. My only intention was to shove one against Laster's skull and fire. For that, I doubted I would need the world's greatest accuracy.

From the Ventura Freeway, I exited at Topanga Canyon and began working the Travato southward across the Santa Monica Mountains. The road was narrow and winding, but I appreciated the canyon's darkness, which afforded some decent stargazing, as well as the chance to collect my thoughts. Unlike the rest of L.A., Topanga seemed to encourage inward reflection, perhaps because there were no flashing lights or marquees.

My plan was beautifully simple: I would knock on Laster's door, explain to whoever answered that I had important information about the investigation into Deliah's death, and then fire a bullet deep into the bastard's brain as soon as he presented himself. Whatever happened after that concerned me not in the least.

. . .

I REACHED Point Dume a little after midnight. I figured Laster would still be awake, knowing his slimy preferences, so I pulled over onto the side of the road a few hundred yards from his estate. With the window blinds drawn shut, I turned on an interior light and removed the two guns from the paper bag.

They were both identical in design—about eight inches in length, metallic silver, with black inlaid handles. The serial numbers appeared to be defaced, as did the name of the manufacturer. All that remained were the numerals "22" engraved on the bases of the handles. I presumed this referred to the caliber of the pistols.

I opened both chambers and determined that the guns were already loaded. It would have been helpful to take a practice shot, but I didn't want to waste time or make any noise, so I stuffed one of the guns under my belt in the small of my back. The other I strapped to my ankle with adhesive tape, just in case. A glance in the mirror confirmed that the devices were unnoticeable, thanks to my outfit of black khaki pants and a gray sport coat.

I was still barefoot from the Cynthia fiasco and I had no other dress shoes with me. It was either sandals, sneakers, or nothing. I settled on nothing, thinking that might connote a greater degree of urgency to whoever opened the door.

All that remained was to fine-tune my psyche. I took a deep breath and recalled my last vision of Deliah as she lay sprawled on her back, her ass and thighs covered with red welts, her clit and nipples swollen from abuse, her eyes and pussy still wide open, yet unable to receive a single input of stimuli.

The bastard was going down.

FOURTEEN

Blinded by the Shadows

THE MASSIVE DOOR opened after one knock. This time an even more petite and nymph-like woman answered. While her facial features appeared vaguely androgynous, her innocent green eyes, full lips, and low-cut dress made it impossible to conceal her femininity.

"May I help you, sir?" she said.

"I need to talk to John. It's urgent."

"I'm afraid Master's not available this evening, sir."

"So is he here or not?"

"Well..." She hesitated.

"Spit it out, bitch," I said, surprising myself. "I'm in no mood to be fucked with."

She stared at me with renewed attention. "He's here, sir, but he's with someone."

"I don't give a shit if he's with Scarlett Johansson. Take me to him or I'll find him myself."

"Yes, sir," she said. "Right this way." She spun around delicately, her long red hair trailing behind her and her scanty dress billowing like a wisp of smoke. I followed her down a corridor embellished with amethyst and aquamarine gemstones of varying sizes.

We entered a small elevator showcasing Egyptian art. Her lips quivered slightly as we descended, but she said nothing and kept her eyes to the ground. The elevator door opened to a dimly lit foyer. I waited for her to exit, but she remained still.

"These are the training grounds," she explained. "I'm not permitted to visit them unless Master requests me."

"And where is he?" I asked.

"I don't know, sir. If you go through the lounge, you'll find an antechamber that leads to four different rooms... depending on Master's mood."

"Fine." I started to exit when she got down on both knees.

"He's going to deny my training because of this," she whimpered. "Will you tell him you forced me, sir?"

"Huh?"

"Will you explain to him that you forced me to help you... so he might forgive me?"

"Sure," I shrugged, as I left the elevator. "I'll explain it to him."

By this point, my eyes had adjusted to the dim light. The lounge was a vast open room, quite similar in layout to The CuntGrind, but decorated far more sumptuously. The floor was covered with a thick Berber carpet, the couches were plush and omnipresent, and elaborate gold frescoes adorned the walls.

I hurried across the space until I found an arched entryway at the rear. It opened to a cave-like vestibule made of Venetian stone. Cautiously, I wound through it until I came upon a series of four doors, spaced about twenty feet apart. Each one was locked tight.

As I debated whether to kick down the doors, I heard Laster's muffled voice issuing from the third room. "Just a little bit more, my slave... show me how deep you can take it."

I positioned my ear to the door so I could hear better. "That's it, slut," continued Laster. "Take it real deep for me. Yeah. That's it." A woman began gagging and coughing. The sound immediately brought forth images of Deliah at her last hour.

"Open up!" I yelled, pounding on the door violently. "It's Wolniak! Open the door now!"

There was a brief moment of silence, followed by a buzzing of the door lock. "*Entrez s'il vous plaît*," said Laster.

I pushed open the door and entered. It was a small, intimate room with an Indian motif. Batiks hung from the ceiling, incense filled the air, and numerous sculptures of Shakti and Shiva provided decoration. A circular bed of red satin occupied the middle of the room.

The platinum blonde who'd greeted me last time was crouched on the floor, wearing nothing but black riding boots and a dog collar. Laster sat on the edge of the bed, working a huge dildo down her throat.

"Welcome to my domain," he said, without turning from his task. "Are you here for some pointers?"

I stepped straight up to him, pulled the gun from under my belt, and pressed it against his temple. "I came to rid the earth of your scumbag brain."

Laster broke out into a smile. "Ah, so that's why you

didn't report me to the cops. You wanted me all to yourself. Very impressive discipline, Paul."

I unlocked the safety and steadied myself to pull the trigger, but I was distracted by the blonde, who continued sucking the dildo. "Take that thing out of her mouth," I demanded.

Laster pushed it deeper as the woman slurped and moaned.

"Take it out, you fucking sadist."

"I must fulfill my contract with my slave." He pulled on her girlish pigtails, tilted her head back, and shoved the dildo further down her throat. The woman gagged again but accepted all that Laster fed her.

"You don't understand," I said gravely. "I'm going to kill you."

"Do it, my friend. If that's your will, I have no intention of resisting. In the meantime, how can I deny my slave what she clearly needs?"

"She doesn't need anything from you."

Laster removed the dildo. "Is that true, Bunni?" he asked her. "You don't need this big thick cock jammed down your throat?"

"Oh yes, I do!" she insisted. "Please feed it to me, Master! I want it as deep as it will go! I need it!"

"You see?" said Laster. "She likes the gun too, don't you, Bunni?"

"Uh-huh!" she enthused. "He can point it at me, Master, if you wish."

"That's entirely up to Paul. He's our Master now."

"Everything's a sick game for you, isn't it?" I countered.

"It's pathetic. You think you can get away with playing games forever. You're sadly mistaken."

"Very well. No more games, Paul. Do what you came here for."

I looked at the woman. "Get out," I ordered her. "You don't need to see this."

She stared at Laster for approval.

"Stay, Bunni," he countered. "Our visitor may kill me, but he certainly won't hurt you. He's too much of a coward to give a slut any pain."

I pointed the gun at Bunni's face. "Get the fuck out of here now."

Laster broke into a bellowing laugh. "All these empty words. What happened to the strong will I thought you had? You're supposed to pull the trigger, not speak for half an hour."

"I said get the fuck out of here! Get the fuck out before I lose it!"

"You've already lost it, my friend," said Laster. "She's not going anywhere. And you certainly don't have the balls to make her go." He paused for effect. "In fact, you know what? I think I feel like fucking Bunni right now. Come here, slut. Get on all fours and spread your cheeks for me. I feel like fucking you in the ass. Hard."

Bunni promptly did as he asked, positioning herself on her knees. She reached back with her hands to spread her smooth white cheeks, as Laster dripped his saliva down her crack. Slowly, he pressed his erect cock into her moistened hole.

"Take it, slave. Take it all the way up your tight ass."

She squealed like an animal as he forced his way inside of her.

I couldn't tolerate any more of this horror show—my head felt like it was about to detach from my neck. I squeezed the trigger furiously and fired into the air. The bullet ricocheted off the ceiling and tore into a sculpture. "Do you see what I'm saying now? Do you?"

Laster continued plowing into her. He didn't even look up at me. Instead, he reached for Bunni's nipples and began to pinch and twist them as he pummeled her. "I'm going to hurt you real good, my little slut," he said.

"Harder!" answered Bunni. "I love it! I love it! I love it!"

Refusing to witness even one more second of the insanity, I fired the gun again, this time straight at Laster's head. His face contracted and I felt sure I hit him squarely, as I was standing just five feet away from him. But then I heard Bunni's yelps and realized my weapon was not true. The barrel must have been skewed from its journey through gangland, causing the bullet to graze her thigh. Blood poured down her leg.

"Fuck yes!" cried Bunni. "Hurt me! Use me! Make me bleed!"

"Jesus Christ," I gasped. "I didn't mean that... I meant it for him." I was breathing so hard, everything in the room started to spin and gyrate.

"We like this, don't we?" said Laster. "Exactly what the doctor ordered."

"I need another cock!" begged Bunni. "Please, sir, fuck me too! Stuff your big cock in my pussy! Use all my holes!" She grabbed my leg and pulled me toward her.

Instinctively, I fired the gun once more, this time into the floor. "Stop it!" I yelled. "Stop it or you'll both die right now!" My words only made them laugh and moan with greater delight.

Laster proceeded to smear Bunni's blood over her body. As he pumped her faster and faster, slapping and defiling her, he pushed his red fingers into her mouth, so she could lick them clean.

"I need more cock!" she squealed while slurping her blood. "I have to feel it! Kill me or fuck me, just give me more cock!" She worked her hands up my trousers, trying to unfasten my belt.

I was stark-raving mad, certifiably mad. With a furious jerk, I pulled away from her, causing her body to detach from Laster and fall to the floor. Barely missing a beat, she flipped onto her back and tucked her legs behind her head, so that he could continue invading her ass.

"Leave her alone!" I shouted at the top of my lungs. "Leave her the fuck alone!" My whole body was quaking and I began bawling like a baby as I fell to my knees.

"If you won't give her more cock, I will," said Laster. He grabbed the huge dildo, rolling it across Bunni's thigh to cover it in blood. Then he pushed the tip of it into her soaking wet pussy while his cock remained inside her ass.

"Aaaaaaaaaaaaaargh!" she groaned in pleasure.

Steadily, he worked the dildo deeper. When the entire twelve-inch shaft filled her pussy, he resumed pumping her ass with his cock. He fucked her with all his might. In and out. In and out. Relentlessly, maniacally, hypnotically.

As he did, Bunni wailed in eerie synchronicity to my own heaving sobs. Her sounds became so desperate and intense, I could no longer hear myself cry. I could no longer determine where my madness ended and hers began. There was no breath in me. No sensory awareness. No bridge from past to future. No presence of mind to reach for the second gun strapped to my ankle.

"Ooooooooooooooooaaaaaaaaaaaaaaaaaaaeeeeeeeehh!" she screeched.

"That's it, slave!" shouted Laster. "We're there now! We're right there! Die for me now! Die for me, my slave!"

With all his bodily force, he thrust himself into her one last time, simultaneously pumping the dildo as hard as he could. Both phalluses, organic and inorganic, penetrated into new unclaimed territory and Bunni's engorged clit expanded to its limit point. She screamed and squirmed, wriggled and whirled as if the end of the world had truly arrived.

And then, at the same moment that Laster withdrew his cock to shoot his load all over her belly, so too did Bunni spray the room with her Amrita, her divine orgasmic fluid. And so too did the swollen vessels of my own temples explode internally, causing me to collapse on the ground as helpless as a newborn—spent, finished, blinded by the shadows of the darkness.

It's Always Been Yours

UNKNOWN HOURS OF BLANKNESS ENSUED. I awoke in such a fog that my eyelids felt fused shut, my brain enveloped by black tar. Had I been buried alive?

Only abject fear powered my eyes to open. When at last I regained my vision, I found I'd been installed in a palatial bedroom filled with rococo Italian furniture. I lay naked on a brass bed. My clothing sat neatly folded on a black lacquered dresser. My two guns rested atop my trousers as if they were perfectly normal appurtenances.

Seeing the weapons spun me into shameful recollection. I tried to push aside my memories of the prior night's activities, but images of Laster and Bunni were burned into my psyche. Like a machete slashing through tender foliage, they could not be denied.

I had no choice but to admit the weakness of my resolve, the enormity of my failure. I was a hollow shell of defeat, a lost soul of idiocy, an utter joke of a man. Laster had eviscerated me and any resemblance to my former self could only be considered superficial.

As I lamented my circumstance, the door to the bedroom cracked open. A young woman entered tentatively—the same red-haired sprite who'd escorted me to Laster's training grounds. She wore a tightly-cropped green blouse and sheer black pants.

"Good morning, sir," she said, placing a tray of food on the bed.

I attempted to sit up to acknowledge her, but a violent head rush vetoed the effort.

"I've prepared your breakfast, sir."

"Ughh," I groaned.

"Were you able to get some sleep?"

"Laster..." I mouthed feebly. "Where is he?"

"Gone for the weekend, sir."

"Shit, fuck, shit."

"Are you okay?" she asked.

"Not exactly."

"You blacked out from exhaustion, sir. Mr. Laster appointed me to nurse you back to health."

She propped me up against my pillow and handed me a glass of cold-pressed watermelon juice. I took a sip, struggling to adjust to the sunlight streaming in from the windows.

"My name is Alex, sir," she continued. "It's short for Alexandra, but you can call me whatever you wish."

I nodded my head imperceptibly, studying the bowl of blueberries on my tray.

"I'm sorry about the confusion last night. I hadn't been

told to expect you." She swayed her exposed belly. "Bunni said you're our best visitor ever. She said you understand energy at a very deep level."

"Ughh."

"I don't mean to hover over you, sir," she blushed. "I can wait in the hallway if you prefer."

"No, stay," I said reflexively.

"Of course, sir."

"Just don't call me sir. Paul will do."

Alex looked crushed. "You don't wish for me to be your sub?"

"No. No, I don't."

"Would you like Bunni to be here instead? She's our resident Tantric goddess. Or one of the other slutgirls?"

"Excuse me?"

"Mr. Laster said you are Master of the house today. All the slutgirls here are for your pleasure... or pain. Whatever you prefer."

"Jesus," I said. "That's insane."

Her lips pouted like a baby. "I'm sorry. You're right. None of us here are good enough for you."

"That's not what I..."

A smile returned to her face and her lips glistened. "So you're not unhappy with me, Master?"

"I'm not unhappy with you, but I have to get going." I pulled myself up out of bed, forgetting that I was naked.

"Oh, sexy Master," she cooed. "You're sooooooo beautiful. May I please dress you, Master?"

"That won't be necessary."

She ran to my side of the bed and knelt in front of me,

her long red hair dangling to the floor. "Please, Master. Please, please, please, please, please. I must serve you."

"Relax, Alex, I'm not going to complain. I promise."

She began softly stroking my calves. "Such a sweet Master. I will only obey you from now on. No one else matters anymore."

I shook my head to discourage her. "No, no, Alex, let's get back to basics here. It's Wednesday morning, am I right?"

"Yes, Master."

"Okay, I have to hurry. I'm expected in the Bay Area tonight."

"Oh, Master," she replied, "I promise I'll be fast." She trailed her smooth lips along my thighs, as she slid my underwear up my legs, guiding it snugly into position. "Mmmm... such a pretty package. Let me get those pants on for you, Master. You see how easy this is?"

Reluctantly, I yielded to Alex's ministrations. She seemed harmless enough, and it had been a long time since someone had tended to me with such devotion. When she finished buttoning my shirt and buckling my belt, I grabbed my sport jacket and gently withdrew from her touch.

"Thank you," I said.

"Don't forget your guns, Master."

"They're Laster's now."

"Are you sure?"

"Yes, very sure. So how do I get out of here?"

"Right this way, Master."

Alex took my hand and led me out of the bedroom. I felt a warm, tingling sensation run through my body, as we descended two flights down a marble spiral staircase. I assumed it was my frazzled nervous system.

When we reached the portico, we were still holding hands. She briefly nestled her body against mine before opening the heavy front door. Then she gestured toward the Solarbeam Yellow roadster, which remained parked in the circular front driveway.

"That's not my vehicle," I said. "Mine's out on the street."

"Bunni moved your RV into the garage," she explained. "I was told to give you this." She handed me the title for the roadster.

"A pink slip?" I said. "I don't understand?"

"The Mercedes is yours, Master. It's always been yours."

I studied the document and saw that she was right. My name showed as the sole owner. Apparently, the vehicle had been registered in my name when Deliah first bought it.

My mind swirled in confusion. I had no interest in keeping the disgusting thing, but I certainly didn't want the bastard to get it either. I would turn it over to Deliah's parents, I resolved. They could sell it for some decent money.

"Where are the keys?" I asked.

"In the cupholder, Master." She got down on her knees again. "May I please come with you? I promise to serve you however you wish."

"No," I replied sternly. "If you want to serve me, make sure nothing happens to my RV. I'll be back for it shortly. Understand?"

"Oh, yes, Master. I understand completely. Thank you so much for letting me help you." She threw her arms around my legs, hugging them tightly. "I'm going to make you so happy, my new Master! So, so happy!"

I waited for Alex to release her hold, not entirely wanting her affection to come to an end. Then I walked outside, averting my eyes, and climbed into the yellow monstrosity.

SIXTEEN

A Done Deal

LIKE A NEWBORN DEER learning to walk, I awkwardly navigated the Mercedes GT R through the residential neighborhood of Point Dume. Everything about the vehicle ill-suited me. Even the seats were uncomfortable. They reminded me of the three-to-a-seat benches in a school bus.

The roadster's seats were wrapped in luxurious leather, but they were rock hard—a fact I'm sure Laster found appropriate. I tried selecting 'Comfort' mode on the over-instrumented control panel, instead of 'Performance' mode, and the effect was about as significant as switching from a bed of nails to one of screws.

To add insult to injury, the exhaust from the roadster produced a cacophonous roar that doubled my headache and caused every human being within a hundred yards to stare at me. Even at five miles per hour, it emitted outrageous revs and cackles like some sort of Beelzebubian teenager. I located a knob that allowed me to adjust the loudness of the exhaust and, surprise, I discovered it was already set to the lowest level.

In other words, I was fucked—royally, supremely, and cosmically. My first thought was to plow the riotous vehicle straight into traffic on the PCH and be done with it all, but the film execs had completed their morning commutes. Not much bang for the buck there.

Besides, I still intended to terminate Laster's life. On this I had not wavered. Yes, my initial attempt had been a colossal failure, but I wasn't a quitter. Far from it. I just needed to recalibrate myself for the second attempt.

My hope was that visiting Deliah's parents in Palo Alto would provide the kick in the pants I sought. I'd load up on Iolana's guilt trips and Walter's inanities while marinating in my grief and sorrow. A day or two in their home would give me all the motivation necessary to finish the job.

In the meantime, avoiding sensory input was my main objective. My aching head shunned all stimuli, so instead of taking the PCH north to Oxnard and hooking up with the 101 freeway—a path that would have meant mountains and beaches and all sorts of other visual distractions—I opted for the monotony of Route 5.

Five hours in the central valley was the perfect antidote. No curves, no steering, no need to interact with the awful vehicle. I was a soulless man in a soulless machine on a soulless road.

Remaining in the right lane, I drove like a grandmother. I sure as hell wasn't interested in feeling the performance of the roadster. Nor did I want to retract the convertible top. The GT R allowed it to be stowed while driving, but I had no desire for more sunlight in my world.

There was already way too much yellow in the cockpit—the designers at Mercedes were obsessed with color coordination. Not only did the roadster's dashboard have yellow leather stitching, but so did the shift knob and the console. Even the seat belts featured the color. Solarbeam Yellow was everywhere.

I blocked it out like a Buddhist monk and maintained my boring speed without any accompaniment. No blaring rock-n-roll, no podcasts, no audiobooks on stress management, and certainly no aggressive lane-changing to gain a coveted car length. I simply stared straight ahead. I knew if my brain were to absorb even one more photon of heinous Solarbeam Yellow, I would spontaneously decombust.

The towns passed by like credits on a movie screen. Lebec, Bakersfield, Lost Hills, Kettleman City. It was startlingly easy to tune out their reality. I kept driving all the way to Tracy. There I stopped for gas, a Big Gulp, and a ninety-nine-cent chicken burger.

If I had to drive a status-screamer like the GT R, I figured I should eat from the lowest trough of society. And it felt right, it felt good. Why feed myself on a higher grade of chow when I hadn't even been able to lodge a bullet into the head of the world's sickest bastard?

After cramming in a last mouthful, I slid back into the shithead mobile and veered west on 580 to make my approach to the Bay Area. Almost instantaneously, the ratio of Teslas increased to the level I was accustomed to in West L.A. All was well with humanity.

Deliah's parents lived in a comfortable part of Palo Alto adjacent to Stanford University. The community housed mostly professors, but in recent years it had seen a steady influx of techies thanks to the area's highly rated schools. Everywhere you looked, homes were being remodeled to new levels of grandiosity.

Walter and Iolana didn't have the spare megabucks to participate in the upgrade game, but their house still passed as sufficiently charming by locals. It was classic Spanish-style with fake adobe walls and plastic terra cotta tile. The home spanned only 4,000 square feet—far too small for Silicon Valley execs—but Walter was an old-timer from Hewlett Packard, so he scored leniency points.

Trained as an engineer, he'd spent most of his career supervising the design of printer cartridges. His particular area of expertise lay in the molding of plastics, but he'd opted for early retirement before salaries went ballistic, meaning his net worth was barely eight figures instead of nine. The discrepancy was a subject of endless discussion for Walter and Iolana.

When I reached their cozy home, the sun was beginning to set. I parked the roadster on the street and walked up to the front door. The last time I'd visited the house without Deliah at my side was on my wedding day. That was six long years ago.

Walter and Iolana greeted me like the world was a place that made sense. We shook hands, exchanged hugs, then they asked the appropriate questions. Was there bad traffic? How long did the drive take? Did I stop along the way? I gave mostly two-word answers.

When the queries ran their course, we moved to the dining table. Walter poured some wine, while Iolana served up homemade poke bowls with the freshest Ahi tuna I'd ever seen. I told her the food looked great, but what caught my eye more was her hair—she'd done it up exactly the way Deliah used to wear hers, in long blonde braids. The similarity was striking.

"What is it?" she said, feeling my stares. "Didn't you know I taught Dee how to fix her hair like this?"

"I... I had no idea," I stammered. "I didn't realize you could look like that too."

"You knew Dee's hair was dyed, right?" interjected Walter.

"Uh, to be honest, I didn't think about it much."

Iolana laughed. "Oh, poor boy. Thought you married a natural blonde."

I started to blush. "Come on, I'm a guy. How am I supposed to understand these kinds of things? I figured she got it from Walter's side of the family."

Walter began to cackle. "Son, I may be pure Swedish, but my bloodline couldn't stand a chance against Iolana's. Dee was born with the darkest hair you ever saw. I mean, really, you think anything blonde would sprout out of skin like hers?"

"That's not the kind of stuff I think about," I babbled. "I loved Deliah for her insides."

"Her insides *and* her outsides were beautiful," replied Iolana. "She was a rare breed, that girl."

"Half Swedish, one-fourth Pacific Islander, and one-fourth African," added Walter.

"What are you talking about?" cried Iolana. "You forgot the Japanese!"

"Oh, yes, yes, I stand corrected."

"In Hawaii, we called ourselves hapa," she said. "But the kids today don't like that term."

"Yeah," I said. "It's a tough time these days."

We all reflected for a moment and I hung my head, realizing I'd just uttered the understatement of the century. None of us could think of what to say next until Iolana happened to look outside the living room window as the street lamps switched on.

"What on earth is that?" she asked, pointing to the roadster. "That's not your car is it, Paul?"

"No," I replied. "I mean, it is, but not really. Deliah put the title in my name, but it was her car. She bought it after the divorce."

"That was Deliah's car?" said Iolana in amazement. "It's so beautiful! Come on, Walter, let's go look at it!"

The two of them rushed outside while I followed behind. They both commented on the lines of the vehicle and hopped inside to test the seats. They even wanted to see the top retract, as Walter had read about it in *Car and Driver*.

"Fantastic," he said, as the top folded itself into the trunk in a matter of seconds. "Simply fantastic. And I say that as an engineer who knows what's involved in that achievement."

"Dee always had good taste," said Iolana. "She really knew how to dazzle."

"If only Hollywood had given her half a chance," said Walter.

"She did very, very well for the short amount of time she had," countered Iolana. "Don't forget that, honey."

"I know, Yo-Yo," he sighed. "We have her whole list of credits framed in the den... for whatever that's worth." He turned to me. "So what're you going to do with the car?"

"I figured I'd sign it over to you. I have no use for it."

"What?" Iolana exclaimed. "We couldn't possibly afford a beauty like that."

"I'm giving it you, not selling it," I explained. "It never really was mine anyway. Deliah bought it with her own money."

"That is so thoughtful, dear," said Iolana. "We'd love to have it... we'd treasure it every day."

"Absolutely," said Walter. "Maybe I'll take it over to Laguna Seca and see what I'm made of. This might be the beginning of that new career I've been looking to jumpstart."

"Oh, please," replied Iolana. "I'm not going to even comment on that."

"What?" he said. "You doubt my prowess behind the wheel? Don't you remember what I was like as a young man?"

She stomped her foot on the ground, letting him know his line of questioning was to come to an end. "Are you sure you really want to do this, Paul?" she asked me.

"I'm sure," I said. "One hundred percent. It's a done deal."

As I spoke the words, the street lamps faded to black up and down the block. I felt a slight resurgence of my soul seeing the SolarBeam Yellow roadster blend into the night. But obviously, it didn't mean a fucking thing.

SEVENTEEN

Another Chance

When we returned inside, Iolana asked if I'd like to look at a scrapbook she'd put together that traced Deliah's life from her first baby steps to her Hollywood career. I politely deferred. The black tar had been receding and I feared the images would cause it to envelop my brain again.

Iolana suggested I retire to the den, which had a decent sofa bed, as their guest room was cluttered with Deliah's personal effects. I crashed out immediately and I slept so deeply that I thought only a few minutes had elapsed. The thick drapes allowed no sunlight to penetrate even at 9 o'clock in the morning.

As soon as I realized I'd overslept, I climbed out of bed and showered—not even pausing to contemplate the shadows. A clarity of mind ran through me, one that had been absent for weeks, if not months or years, and I didn't want to do anything to jinx it. No heavy eyelids, no throbbing headache. I couldn't speculate why.

For breakfast, we ate Belgian waffles with strawberries and

maple syrup. Festivity in the face of loss was a coping strategy favored by Walter and Iolana. I went along with it to the best of my ability and my head remained surprisingly pain-free.

After trading a few more trivialities, the subject of the scrapbook came up again. I didn't even flinch. Iolana brought me the book to review and I started to lift open the heavy bound cover, but before I could she screeched with delight.

"I just thought of the most wonderful idea! You need to take some pictures of Dee's new Mercedes so I can add them to the scrapbook!"

"Yes, yes," replied Walter. "That's a very good idea."

"You could do that morphing thing!" suggested Iolana.

"I'm not sure what you mean," I replied.

"You know, to make it look like Dee is inside her Mercedes. Don't you do that kind of stuff at your work? Take a picture and put it inside another picture?"

"Blending images? Yes, that's pretty easy with the right software. But we'd need a good image of her, preferably in a seated pose."

"Not a problem," said Walter. "I've got the latest version of Photoshop and Iolana has thousands of pictures. I'm sure she can find the perfect one." He softly patted the scrapbook.

"Sounds like a plan," I said.

"Time to earn your keep," he continued. "Let's see that graphics wizardry you're so famous for."

Walter produced a new Canon digital camera, showing off its array of features, and we headed out to the roadster. Because of my former position at MediaCow, he was convinced I must be an accomplished photographer, so he pushed the camera into my hands. I didn't see the point of explaining that I worked from my own sketches, not from externally-generated images.

Fortunately, setting the camera in auto-mode made it pathetically simple to operate. I studied the sun and decided that the best approach would be a bird's-eye view of the driver's side with the top down. If it were my scrapbook, I would have chosen a shot of the roadster entirely obfuscated by shadow, but why be difficult?

I grabbed a step ladder from their garage, positioning it about ten yards from the vehicle, while Walter lowered the top. Then I climbed up the ladder, captured the whole illuminated yellow mess in the viewfinder, and snapped the photo. Hooray.

Walter led me back to his computer and we downloaded the image onto his hard drive. I opened it in Photoshop and we agreed it was a decent shot of the vehicle. The composition would nicely accommodate an image of Deliah at the wheel.

"Yo-Yo!" Walter yelled, "Did you pick out a photo?"

"Yes, honey." She entered the room with two glossy photos in her hand.

"Great," I said. I couldn't see the images because of my position behind the computer—and I didn't feel compelled to turn around to look at them.

"I hope it's okay that they're prints," she added.

"We're old-school," explained Walter.

"No worries," I replied, "that's what scanners are for."

"So which one should we use?" she asked.

"You choose," Walter replied. "I only have expertise in pictures of myself."

"Oh, please," she gasped. "How about this one?" She handed me her choice.

I took one look at the image and everything inside of me crumbled as if a violent chemical reaction were occurring within me. I felt kinetically altered, my body transformed at a cellular level. And yet somehow I remained seated.

The photograph showed a close-up of Deliah sitting on our four-poster bed. Her long blonde hair was kinked wildly from curlers and she wore an uncharacteristically mischievous grin, one that suggested she harbored some secret knowledge of another world. But it was her eyes that crumbled me. I could feel them staring straight into me, straight into my uncluttered mind, with no pretense, no illusion, no barriers of hurt and rejection.

I was the one who'd taken the photo and the memory of that day came flooding back to me. For whatever reason, in that instant, the impenetrable distance between us had temporarily lifted. It was the last time we'd been that close.

Deliah's mask of protection had been stripped clean and, in reducing herself like that, she'd reduced me. I could see clear as day what had attracted me to her in the first place. More importantly, I could see what she'd been attracted to in me—and it was not a man fiddling with Photoshop to please her parents, of that I was certain.

"What's the matter? Is something wrong?" asked Iolana.

"Paul? Paul? Are you all right?" said Walter.

I heard them speaking. I could feel them next to me, waiting for me to do something with the photo, waiting for me to respond to them as a normal, predictable member of the human race. But I remained in my crumbled state, unable to form words. Thoughts swirled to the surface of my consciousness from crevices within me I did not recognize and I simply let them bubble and percolate.

How much longer would I be a lost soul wandering the earth? How much longer would I hide behind the riskless farce of no conviction, no experience, no knowledge, no position, no belief, no power, no resolve, no future? I was worse than a joke. I was an emasculation.

Why hadn't I realized it earlier? Deliah had given *me* the roadster. She'd wanted me to have it for a reason. It was a gift from her freed soul. She didn't give it to me so that I could run back to her parents and soothe them into a numb complacency while the world frothed in unbounded possibility.

The roadster was a device made for living. To taste what is. Outside the parameters of what one should or should not do. To decide for oneself. That was why she bought it. That was why she bought it for me. It was never meant for her use. It was meant for *my* use.

The exalted but defiant persona of the vehicle—the persona I so despised—was exactly what Deliah had desired to free herself from her shackles. It was exactly what she'd sought to unearth within her husband, exactly what I'd failed to give her. And it was exactly why she went to Laster. Not to discard me, but to guide me.

It had nothing to do with betrayal and nothing to do with sexuality. How fucking shallow of me to assume such trivialities were the issue. Her lesson was as transparent as the GT R's windshield. The object of life was not to live as long as one possibly could. The object was to live to the fullest extent possible, even if for only one second.

Deliah had already done so, whether my ego could face

it or not. And now she was giving me another chance. A chance I did not entirely deserve. But if I failed to take it, then I was thoroughly unredeemable. Then I was beyond redemption. I was more dead than death itself. I was so dead that not even the shadows would take me.

EIGHTEEN

Not Good Stuff

JUDGING from the confused looks on Walter and Iolana's faces, I must have been in my fugue for an appreciable amount of time, perhaps two or three minutes. When I emerged, Iolana scurried to get me a glass of water and Walter plied me with all manner of questions. But I had no desire to offer an explanation, nor did I feel I owed one. I only wanted to set the record straight regarding the GT R.

"I've changed my mind," I announced. "I've got to go." Walter and Iolana followed me, as I went to gather my belongings from the guest room.

"Did we do something wrong?" said Iolana. "Walter can be rude sometimes without knowing it."

"I realized I need the roadster," I explained.

"Are you serious?" asked Walter.

"You had us so excited," added Iolana.

"Sorry, it turns out I have to drive it. Now." I hurried downstairs, heading for the front door.

"Well, you damn well better bring it back, son. A gift is a gift."

"And what about the morphing?" Iolana called out. "You're still going to do that, aren't you?"

"Don't know," I replied, my head thumping in a new way. "We'll just have to see. Thanks for everything."

I exited the house with my bag slung over my shoulder, as Walter and Iolana trailed behind in confusion. The roadster looked entirely different than it had earlier that morning. Evidently, I'd been reborn because it now looked like a god damn masterpiece.

Its curvaceous yellow lines, full yet sleek, reminded me of the way Deliah's blonde braids fell down her back when she lounged in bed. The front grille evoked her beckoning smile, the rear spoiler her swooped back. I practically wanted to fuck the car.

So complete was my transformation, I sprinted to the vehicle and leaped over the side door as if I were some sort of caped hero. Walter and Iolana stared out at me, their mouths hanging wide open, but I didn't care. I paused to stroke the Nappa leather of the driver's seat before I drew the Solarbeam Yellow seat belt across my chest. Then I pushed the ignition.

Instantly, the velvet purr of the engine came to life. I jammed the shifter into drive and pumped the gas pedal hard. The roadster responded with a momentary squeal before the fat tires caught the road and I was hurled forward at a seemingly impossible rate of acceleration.

Blaring the horn and waving goodbye, I achieved forty miles per hour in under two seconds. I yearned to keep my foot on the aluminum-clad gas pedal, but a stop sign loomed.

I applied the brakes and guided the supercharged beast to a stop before resuming toward El Camino Real, the main surface street cutting through Palo Alto.

At the onramp to the 101 Highway South, I gunned the engine again. The speedometer rocketed to seventy before I even merged with traffic, but the GT R only hummed. I swerved into the fast lane and selected 'Performance' mode. Before I knew it, my speed topped a hundred and the roar of the exhaust sounded like Rachmaninoff.

The mix of sound, wind, and light made me ache to push the car harder, but I knew better than to let loose in the city. Visions of hairpin turns on Route 1 in Big Sur flickered through my mind. Mountains and oceans were exactly what I needed. Bring on the sensory data.

As I veered onto Highway 17, I allowed myself to explore the interior appointments. I'd barely interacted with the car on the ride up, but now I found myself fingering each of the buttons on the steering wheel and the instrument cluster. I studied every function, every switch, every control until the GT R felt like an extension of myself.

I reached over to the glove box and rifled through the contents—an owner's manual, a tire pressure gauge, some receipts, a pair of sunglasses. Cruising at a cautious eighty-nine miles per hour, I opened the covered compartment in the center console. Deliah's cell phone sat inside.

Holding the phone in my hand, I replayed in my mind the countless hours she'd been glued to it. Her phone was her lifeline to Hollywood. When it rang, everything else came to an immediate halt in the hopes that maybe, just maybe, it was *the* call.

On a whim, I redialed the last outbound number.

Maher's secretary answered immediately. When I told her who I was, she transferred the call.

"Yeah?" said Maher.

"I need to know something," I said reflexively.

"Fire away."

"Why'd you title the GT R in my name?"

"Deliah asked me to, Pauly. I didn't think you'd mind another 200k in assets." He laughed loudly. "She paid cash, you know, so there's no liability. Besides, I figured you deserved it. Least she could do after all her bullshit."

"And the reason you didn't tell me before?"

"Part of our agreement. She didn't want you to know and I knew better than to ask why. I was just glad to be righting the score in your favor."

"Uh-huh."

"I couldn't help telling you about the license plate in advance, so you'd see what a vain bitch she was."

"You don't need to call her a bitch, Gene," I said softly.

"Oh, please. Don't tell me you love her again now that she left you a fucking Mercedes."

"What else haven't you told me?"

"Oh, Pauly. Pauly, Pauly, Pauly."

"What else? Come on. I know there's more." My voice tensed up a few notches.

"Just let it go, buddy. Let it fucking go."

"If you really want to help me, you'll tell."

"It's not good stuff," he said tentatively.

"Let me explain something," I replied. "I'm not angry at my wife anymore. I used to be, but that's over. Way over. The choices Deliah made are not for me to judge. I'm sure she had her reasons. Now I just want to give her spirit what I couldn't give her body. You understand?"

"No, not really. To be honest, it sounds like you could use a little therapy. You know, some couch time does a body good."

"Stop hiding in your bullshit humor, Gene. You'll be facing death soon enough yourself. It may be too scary for you to admit, but for all essential purposes, you're already dead now. Your whole fucking day in the office, on the phone, at court, on the freeway... that is a dead day. And guess what? You damn well know you're dead. You simply choose not to live. That's fine. I couldn't care less what your stupid-ass demons are. But, personally, I'm deciding to live now. So don't think I'm going to flip out over some information that's 'not good stuff.' I'll dig a whole lot fucking deeper than that with or without your help."

"Jesus, buddy. Chill. You want to hear it, fine. It's no skin off my back."

"Thank you."

"Deliah did some adult work for a company based in Cyprus."

"You mean videos?" I asked.

"Yes, but very hardcore stuff, Pauly. Too hardcore to release on mainstream sites. That's why the company's based in Cyprus, to cover their asses in case of obscenity charges or some shit like that."

"How long did she work for them?"

"I'm not sure. I believe it was something she got into fairly recently. Her payment stubs were only for this year. She wanted me to hide her earnings in case you asked for documentation during the discovery period, but you never asked for shit so it didn't matter."

"Okay."

"She really, really didn't want you to know about it. I don't know why I'm letting you get it out of me so fucking easily. She said it would kill you."

"It would have killed the old me, but not the new me. Not now. Not in the least."

"Not sure what to make of that, but duly noted."

"I don't care what you make of it, Gene. Just tell me the name of the site."

"Oh, hell, I have no idea."

"Bull fucking shit. You checked it out, Gene. Hardcore porn. Give me a break. You're all over that shit. That shit is designed for lawyers like you."

Maher laughed. "Man, I don't know what's happened to you, but I sort of like it, I have to say."

"So tell me the name. Then I'll leave you alone and you can go back to dying."

He laughed again, even harder. "You've become a fucking dangerous dude, Pauly. Have you thought about starting a cult or something?"

"Come on. The URL. Tell me."

"All right, all right, Pauly. This is the only other thing I know, got that? There's nothing else, okay? But contrary to your analysis, I'm not a hardcore man. The stuff is pretty sick... I barely looked at two or three clips and then I was out of there. So you've been warned, all right? I told you it's not good stuff, and if I give it to you then I expect you to stay true to your new tough-guy posture and suck it in like a man."

"Understood, Gene. Don't you worry about me."

"Let me think for a sec," he said hesitantly. "I'm trying to remember, hmmm... oh, okay, pretty easy. It's painsluts.com. Got that? Pain-Sluts-Dot-Com."

NINETEEN

Pure Life Force

THIS WAS GOOD. So fucking good. Even in the stop-and-go traffic of Carmel, I could feel the roadster's dual-clutch transmission meshing with my impulses. The synchronization far exceeded my PCP-induced experiences in my old Honda Civic.

It had nothing to do with gaining outward attention. Carmel was littered with rich seductresses flashing me smiles, but I hardly needed their validation. If I wanted one of them, I'd simply indicate my wish and the deed would be done. I'd certainly never hold back again like I had with Cynthia. What a pathetic joke.

That was exactly why I'd lost Deliah. All those years I'd cared so much about other people's image of me. I'd thought it was a sign of weakness to rely on money and power to prop up oneself.

In reality, the weakness had been in me. How convenient to blame the system, to blame materialism, for my own shortcomings. I was simply scared. Scared to embrace the unknown. Scared to live life to the fullest. Scared to be honest about what I truly desired. No wonder I'd immersed myself in shadows. Darkness cooperated nicely with my inner deceit.

The roadster, on the other hand, was purely about light. There was nothing lurking in its shadow. It cried out its essence to all onlookers equally. The hotties parading on the sidewalks knew exactly who I was as soon as they saw me driving the Solarbeam Yellow sex toy. With one glance, they computed that I would give them the fuck of their lives. And they were right, I would.

But I had no interest in brats, at least not the generic variety. Maybe if they were into spanking. Maybe if they were suitably deferential. Maybe, maybe, maybe. I needed more time with the roadster to fully map my plan. There was painsluts.com to consider, not to mention my unfinished business with Alex.

Whatever I did, I wasn't going to waste any more of my life with incomplete action. It was all or nothing now. Just as I intended to push the roadster to its limit, so too did I plan to ride the female species to the furthest plane of ecstasy. Every fantasy, every dream, every lustful thought I now vowed to pursue with reckless abandon—or else I would die without Deliah's sanctity.

To hell with Carmel though. The city elders had outlawed street addresses in a bid for charm, but it only demonstrated their preference for veneer over depth. Even the teenage girls limited their rebellions to dyed hair and pierced bellies—no deeper, no further within their pampered bodies. Yet their insides were what most needed the light.

So when the traffic at last dissipated, I stepped on the gas and rocketed to a hundred and twenty miles per hour. Within minutes, the overcrowded city gave way to coastal foothills covered with wildflowers. I spotted Point Lobos in the distance, confirming that my ride had begun in earnest.

The highway was almost vacant, the tourists all busy buying knick-knacks. I accelerated with every straightaway and tested the roadster's response with every curve. The harder I pushed, the more its speed-sensing steering reassured me—even the rear wheels turned when needed.

As I approached Big Sur, the precipices became steeper, the ocean views more dramatic, and the turns more severe. Still, the GT R matched my every action with perfect obedience. No matter what decision I made, no matter what request I made, it complied willingly.

A brief clearing allowed me to nudge the speedometer to one thirty. I saw a tight s-turn approaching and resisted slowing until the last possible moment. The roadster swallowed the corner with ease, seemingly laughing at my concern. Even the ceramic brakes whispered a confidence, a conviction that I could depend on them, that the vehicle would remain rock-steady.

I yearned to go faster—to find out what the roadster would offer in lieu of control. Where would it stand when warm, fuzzy security was replaced with cold, hard uncertainty? If I didn't know that, how could I move forward with confidence? It would be just another shaky relationship culminating in breakup.

"Make this engine feel some hurt!" I screamed into the wind. I pulled out of the s-turn and punched the accelerator into the straightaway. The turbocharger complied, serving up 7,500 RPMs without hesitation.

I raced toward the next bend, my hair flying, the cobalt sea looming below and the azure sky above. The roadster throbbed gutturally, showing no reluctance. With a maniacal grin, I dialed the exhaust setting to its loudest level and jammed the pedal to the floor. The tailpipe released a whoop of exaltation.

Preparing for my turn, I drifted into the oncoming lane— no traffic, right?—and forced the transmission into third gear. The engine redlined, but the angelic cry of the exhaust gave sweet reassurance. Barely decelerating, the roadster cut the corner like butter.

I gleefully pushed forward into a straight patch. Faster, faster, faster. One forty. One fifty. One sixty. A narrow bridge spanning two canyons approached, but I felt no compulsion to reflect on its engineering.

Spectacular vistas were every which way, as the road carved through the mountainside. Pelicans dove for bounty amidst churning whitewater. Waterfalls culminated on pristine beaches. Ferns adorned cloud-moistened canyons.

Suddenly, a human handiwork leaped to my attention amidst the splendor. Marked on a giant rock protruding from the ocean-side of the highway was a single word in bright yellow spray paint: DELIAH.

While cornering at one thirty-five, I slammed on the brakes, not thinking of the consequences. The roadster wailed furiously, the rear wheels unable to avoid slippage. I strained to engage the ABS, but the vehicle remained untamed, skidding across the pavement.

By dumb luck, the shoulder was wider than usual along that portion of the road, although only a flimsy guardrail stood between it and the sheer cliffside. I glanced at the speedometer—eighty-five miles per hour. The smell of burnt rubber dominated my senses.

This was the test I sought. How to regain control and avoid direct impact with the guardrail? My blood pounded in excitement, not fear, and I noticed a strange tinkling sound behind my right ear. Instinctively, I turned into the skid, though I'd never understood the physics of such a move.

The roadster responded by reducing the excess power to the drive wheel, thanks to the AMG traction control and the dynamically enhanced handling. I was only inches from the guardrail now, but my speed plummeted to thirty-five. Easy peasy.

One flick of my wrist and the GT R veered away from the guardrail. Problem solved. I let out a slight hoot and pulled over at the next turn-out.

With the engine running, I hopped out of the vehicle to take inventory. A cursory inspection of the body showed not even a scratch. The roadster gleamed like nothing had happened. Not a single other car was in sight.

After catching my breath, I walked back up the road a few hundred feet toward the graffiti-marked rock. A long skid mark proved the reality of the event. And there it was again in plain view: DELIAH.

I studied the yellow marking and wondered if it could possibly refer to my Deliah. The letters were crude and rough, not unlike what I would expect from the portly whip master at the CuntGrind. And so?

So this was fucking good. Here I was on the coastline of Big Sur and everything was unfolding as it should. The sun was shining, the roadster was humming, and I was breathing oxygen. So very fucking good.

As I returned to the vehicle, I remembered the strange tinkling sound I'd heard. Perhaps something had come loose from the violent skidding? I checked the roadster's rear wing, as well as the padding around the roll bars, but everything seemed secure. Then I noticed a leather pocket behind the driver's seat.

I reached inside and extracted the cause of the tinkling— a black leather dog collar with a silver chain leash. Both the chain and the collar were encrusted with alternating amethyst, citrine, and aquamarine gemstones.

The adornment was intended for Deliah, obviously. I wondered how many Doms had fastened the collar around her smooth neck while taking her for their pleasure. Just Laster? A dozen others? Who the hell knew?

I decided it made no difference—I was done with jealousy forever. The important thing was that I'd passed the test. On a leap of faith, I'd left the realm of control and let the universe dictate the outcome.

The result was an injection of pure life force energy. For the first time, I held out hope that my trauma might not determine my future. The collar symbolized liberation, not servitude.

Staring down at the vastness of the ocean, I cried tears of joy. I cried and cried and cried, my tears dripping seaward down the cliff. Water to water, light to light, shadow to shadow. Good was everywhere—so much good it could not be contained.

Good and only good.

TWENTY

The Wait for the End

AFTER DRYING my eyes and cruising a few miles southward, I stopped for a late lunch at Nepenthe. The view from the outdoor patio was boringly spectacular, as were the literary waitresses. Significance abounded in every direction, along with the promise of Samadhi, but I'd had enough of luring landscapes and high-brow redemption scenes. The shallow surfaces of L.A. held more appeal. It was time to be true in the land of illusion.

On the drive south, I contemplated Laster and my misplaced rage. Of all my projections, all my mistakes and errors, that was the granddaddy. Laster's words and actions had revealed nothing ulterior. No pomp, no subterfuge, no ego. And it had burned me up inside. What gave him the right to bypass the churning complexities of life?

I laughed aloud, thinking of my escapade with the hand-guns. It perfectly mirrored my flawed effort at existence. Only upon loving death would I become alive. This I now understood, perhaps not as fully as Laster, but still I understood. Death was the most goodness there could be. Death was the only real goodness. Death was what the shadows sought, but what they could never hope for, try as they might.

The problem was managing the wait *until* death. My idea of wandering the continent in an RV seemed laughable at this point, as did avenging Delilah, and I had no intention of returning to MediaCow or any other design job. But I couldn't very well sleep in the roadster. The Travato still made practical sense.

A few hours of easy driving landed me back at Point Dume. I arrived in the twilight hour, just as I had one day earlier. The sight of the enormous estates occupying the neighborhood didn't turn my stomach quite as much this time around.

Winding down Birdview Avenue to Cliffside Drive, I almost felt whole. My heart pumped rhythmically, as I pulled into Laster's driveway and parked behind a forest green Land Rover. If the opportunity presented itself, I resolved to humbly apologize to Laster before retrieving the Travato and going my merry way.

Bunni opened the front door the moment I climbed out of the roadster. "Hello, sir!" she cried out in a bubbly voice. "We've missed you terribly!"

"Hi, Bunni," I replied. "How's your leg healing?"

"Awesome, it's going to make a beautiful scar!"

"Glad to hear it," I said. "Is John home?"

"He's in New York for the day, but he told us we should make you feel at home. Please come in, sir."

"Actually, I just stopped by for my RV."

"Of course," she said. "It's in the garage. I'll tell Rudy to open it for you."

"Thank you. Do you think it'd be all right to leave my Mercedes here until I get settled, just for a day or so?"

"Of course, sir. You're our favorite visitor, don't you know?" She giggled.

"I appreciate it."

"Master Laster appreciates you too!"

As I walked to the garage, the door to the fourth bay opened. It was walled off from the rest of the garage and quite spacious, measuring about fifteen feet wide and fifty feet deep. Its interior boasted skylights and a large rear window with a panoramic view of the ocean.

The Travato was parked in the center. Although dwarfed by the enormity of the bay, it looked to be freshly washed and waxed. I opened the driver's door and climbed inside the cab. It was sparkling clean.

Turning back to peer into the living area, I saw Alex sitting cross-legged on the bed, wearing nothing but one of my dress shirts unbuttoned to the waist. Her eyes were closed peacefully and her red hair cascaded down her back to the comforter. Like the cab, the camper was immaculate and I detected the scent of orange blossoms.

"Hello, Alex," I said.

She slowly opened her eyes and smiled. "Hello, my dear Master. Did you have a good trip?"

"Yes, actually I did."

"I'm so glad, Master." She parted her shirt to reveal her perfectly mounded breasts and trimmed pubic hair. "I've been thinking about you constantly."

"It looks like you did some spring cleaning," I said.

"I did it naked."

"And now you're wearing my shirt?"

"I ached to feel your essence, Master," said Alex. "Do you want me to take it off?"

I studied her for a moment. "Yes, take it off," I finally said.

She removed the shirt and got up to hang it in the closet.

"You don't need to bother with that," I said. "There are more important tasks."

"Mmmm... yes, Master."

I reached for her, planting a forceful kiss on her lips. She reciprocated hungrily and we fell to the bed. She landed on her back with her legs spread and her knees upward. One of her hands began to tease her nipples, as the other slid up her milky thighs and parted her pussy lips. I could see her pink labia pierced by two silver hoops.

"I'll do anything you ask, Master," she said. "I want to give you every part of myself."

"Every part?"

"Yes, every, every part. You own me now, Master. I ache to please you."

My cock twinged with excitement in a way I'd never before felt. I owned Alex? Why not? Whom would it harm?

"Let's see you on all fours," I said. "Show me your cute little bottom."

She rolled over onto her hands and knees, obediently pushing her butt cheeks up in the air for me. "Mmm, I love this, Master."

"Use your hands to show me more, Alex."

"Yes, Master." She reached for both cheeks and slowly spread them apart, taunting me. "Do you like what you see? Are you going to fuck me in my tight little ass, Master?"

"It depends on if you deserve it or not," I said, surprised that the words came out of me. "Your pussy and ass will each have to earn my cock."

"Oooh, Master! You get me so excited when you say that!"

I stood up and walked toward the bed, as she twisted around to face me. Our eyes locked for several seconds, then I pulled her to me and kissed her again. She reciprocated while struggling to remove my shirt and jeans. I held her tightly, cradling her head, pressing against her breasts, and pushing my tongue deep into her mouth.

When she finally managed to unzip my pants, her hands reached inside my briefs for my hardening cock. "Please let me suck it," she said. "Please, please, please, Master. I need to taste it."

"You may," I replied, "but only if you promise to make it harder than it's ever been. I want you to give yourself to the task completely and serve my cock for as long as you can. Worship it like it is your highest god. If you're very, very good, I might fuck you, Alex."

She whimpered slightly and I could see my words had struck a chord. Like a geisha, she stripped me of my remaining clothes. Her tongue tenderly worked its way from my neck to my chest to my belly, then darted down to my loins, until at last it flickered across the tip of my cock.

Slowly and devotedly, she began to fellate me in a manner I had not known possible. It felt as if she had complete access to the map of my neural networks. With uncanny precision, she intuited the exact response in my brain to each of her actions.

She licked softly first, focusing only on the tip. When my cock swelled, she extended her coverage to the head, using both her tongue and fingertips, circling round and round, adding more pressure little by little. Each time I approached the apex of my need, she abruptly stopped, only to resume her efforts once again.

Just as I thought I could tolerate no more, she paused to stare deep into my eyes, then pushed my member into her mouth. She began gyrating her head up and down, again and again—sometimes fast, sometimes slow. Yet she always remained in perfect control, sensing exactly when to stop, when to continue, when to slow the wave of pleasure and when to accelerate it, so that each cycle took me higher and higher and higher.

For the better part of an hour, she nursed my organ in this manner, as I lay in suspended rapture. Before I could even think where I yearned to feel her lips and tongue, she anticipated my need and fulfilled it. My request for her to make my cock harder than it had ever been seemed almost trivial, so easily did she deliver me to new levels of turgidity.

When she could tell I was approaching my furthest edge, she responded by squeezing my cock and holding perfectly still. "Do you want to make your slutgirl gag?" she asked in a high-pitched voice. She waited for several seconds, ignoring my stunned silence. Her throat opened wide for me and I could feel its warm wetness slowly wrapping around the full length of my shaft all the way to its base.

Excited by her submission, and even more so by my acceptance of it, she continued to coax my organ deeper and deeper down her throat. When at last she took it all within her, she made a delicate gagging and choking sound, almost as if she were singing and cumming at the same time. She made one final push, guiding my balls inside her mouth, before delicately withdrawing and dripping her saliva all over my genitalia.

I knew I had to take her immediately or I would orgasm before I had the chance. Desperately, I pushed her tiny frame off my cock and onto her back. "Does the slut's pussy need to be fucked now?" I asked in a quivering voice. I spread her legs as wide as they would go, while my aching cock rubbed against her hard clit.

"Ooooh, yes, please fuck me, Master!" she cried.

My cock felt so intensely energized, I could scarcely discern it from the rest of my body—or anything else for that matter. The whole Travato throbbed, pounded, and vibrated. Everything was sex. Sex was everything. There were no constraints, no darkness. Nothing existed but pure pleasure and light.

"Beg for it, slave," I demanded. "Show me how badly you want it." I tapped her pussy lips with my engorged limb.

"Please, Master, I beg you! Please push your beautiful hard cock deep into my soaking wet pussy! I'll do anything, Master, please!"

"Beg for me to fuck you."

"Oooh yes, Master, please fuck me!" she moaned. "Please fuck my pussy! Fuck me, fuck me, fuck me, Master, please!"

Ever so slowly, I pushed my cock—just the very tip—into her slit. It felt like wet silk, so moist and soft and pure. My entire being craved more, but instead I pulled back and rested my cock on her belly. "Is that enough, slave?"

"More, Master! Please fuck me more, I'm begging you, I have to have it, Master! Please, I need it!"

Guided by an inner passion I did not know I had, I slipped inside her further, then pulled the tip back out. In again, then out again. In and out. In and out. Each time I entered only a millimeter deeper and I only let her feel the sensation for a brief moment.

Alex gasped and sighed with desire, but I did not stop my teasing. "I own your pussy now," I said commandingly. "I can use it any way I want."

"Yes, Master, you own it," she replied. "It's yours completely, however you want to use it, whenever you want to use it. It's always yours."

When she spoke her words of affirmation, I couldn't restrain myself. There was no chance of hesitation on my part, unlike my encounter with Cynthia. I took a deep breath and rammed my cock inside her.

"Yes! That's it!" she shouted. "That's it!"

I held my throbbing cock inside her for several seconds, then I pulled out and pounded her another time—hard, deep, and fast. I pumped her again and again and again. Over and over and over. Each stroke felt more complete, more divine, more all-encompassing than I'd dared to believe was possible. Until I felt the next one.

I climbed so high with Alex, I abandoned the rational side of my brain altogether, surrendering to some unnamed part of myself over which I knew I had no dominion. Yet my wild frenzy did not frighten her in the least. It only made her wail louder in delight, begging to give her still more, aching for an ever-deepening union.

"Now take me from behind, Master!" she pleaded. "Use me every way you can!"

I complied gratefully, flipping her onto her hands and knees. She began playing with her nipples again, this time pinching them between her fingertips. My hands spread apart her ass cheeks, as I worked my cock inside her pussy.

"Yes, open me up!" she cried. "As deep as you can, I need it!"

To my delight, I found I could plumb even greater depths from this angle. And still, I craved more. I ached to fill her to saturation, to pleasure her to her limits.

"I'm going to spank your cute little ass now," I said. "I'm going to make it turn bright red." The words were pouring out of me from a part of myself I did not know.

"Yes, Master!" Alex squealed. "Spank me! Discipline me!"

I opened my right palm and gently patted her ass. My cock twinged and hardened, much as it had when I'd spanked Cynthia. But now I had no misguided guilt, no faulty transference or projection.

"More, Master! More!"

I tapped her a little harder, once on each ass cheek. Alex groaned in pleasure. "Please, Master! Spank my ass!"

Her buttocks had a firm, yet creamy smooth texture. I truly could not get enough of them. As my cock continued fucking her from behind, I raised my hand and bore down harder on her right cheek.

"Yes! Yes, Master!"

The stinging sensation on my hand led me into

rapturous bliss. My cock swelled beyond recognition and I could feel Alex's pussy contracting in excitement. I *had* to spank her again. I pumped her with my cock twice, then smacked her squarely on both cheeks.

"Oh, God, yes! Harder, Master! Harder!"

Her ass was starting to glow bright red. I softly massaged it and then—smack, smack, smack—my firm hand struck her again. I delivered the blows crisply and soundly as if I'd been engaged in this sort of activity for years. It felt like a redemption, an absolution, like entering a new world for which I had been preparing unknowingly all my life.

"Fuck yes! I need it, I need it so fucking bad! Do it, Master! Make it sting, make it hurt!"

Alex's pussy was a river now. I could feel her juices dripping onto my balls. She was so completely open, I was able to slide my cock still deeper inside her.

I raised my hand again and bore down all the way, directly on her quivering ass cheek. Whump! My hands left a mark, yet she only squirmed in pleasure. I wanted to use my slut to her greatest capacity. My cock was on fire.

Whump! Whump! Whump! It was incredible. It was impossible. It was exactly what we both wanted. What we both needed. What we both had to have. I was the Master, she was the submissive, and we were equals, total equals.

Whump! Whump! Whump! With each spanking that I administered, Alex wailed in ecstasy, crying out for more, begging for harder strikes and deeper pounding. The combination of pleasure and pain, of giving and receiving, was like a narcotic—she had to take it, I had to give it.

I slammed her pussy once more with a giant thrust and smacked her ass as hard as I could. WHUMP!!! The feeling flooded through me to my core. She screamed and wailed, gyrated and bucked, and I knew we had both reached the other side.

"I'm cumming, Master! I'm cumming!"

Reflexively, without thinking, I pulled out of her and shouted I was going to cum too. Alex spun around beneath me and positioned herself in front of my throbbing cock. There was no way to delay my response a second longer. I came and came and came in tremendous arcing spurts that landed all over her mouth and face and hair.

As she struggled to swallow every drop, I felt enveloped by an overarching sensation of acceptance—an acceptance that radiated through every fiber of my being. The wait for the end no longer concerned me in the least. I now understood how I would spend my time.

At last, it all made perfect fucking sense.

TWENTY-ONE

Privileged White Cis Male

THE NEXT MORNING, I awoke in a state of undeniable perfection. Alex lay nestled in my arms with her head resting on my chest. Her satin skin felt like a blanket sent from the gods. I couldn't remember ever being so relaxed, so calm, so fulfilled.

I soaked in her essence, remaining entirely still, and listened to her breathing for almost an hour. Ordinarily, my mind would have been whirring with a million thoughts and distractions, but with Alex in my bed, I was able to stay grounded in the experience. There was nothing else I wanted to do, nowhere else I wanted to be.

When she began to stir, I almost felt disappointment, as I yearned for the magic of our connection to continue. Then I realized it didn't have to end. Her mere existence was all I needed to keep it going.

"Master?" she sighed. "You're still here? You didn't leave?"

"I'm still here," I said, stroking her hair.

"I'm so glad… but, oh…" She looked up at me like her world had suddenly fallen into a deep, dark pit.

"What's wrong? What is it?"

"I wasn't prepared for this… I never expected…" Her eyes started to tear.

"You never expected what?"

"That you'd still be here… that I would feel this way… that things between us would unfold like this."

"It's okay," I soothed her. "Everything's okay."

"No, it's not," she said. "I screwed up. I totally screwed up."

"I don't see how you can say that."

"I wish somehow you could understand, but I know it's not possible. I've been so alone. I wouldn't have done it if I hadn't felt so terribly alone. I know that's no excuse."

"Done what?" I pleaded. "Done what?"

"Not told you. I should have told you right from the start. It was selfish and stupid. I had this crazy fantasy that things could be different this time. For once, I thought maybe things could be different. I'm so stupid…"

I took a deep breath, still not comprehending. *What* hadn't she told me? My stomach was in knots, bracing for the worst. But I was determined not to lose my composure. I kept telling myself to remember how good I felt when I woke up— her smooth skin pressed up against mine. Whatever she hadn't told me, I resolved not to forget that feeling.

"I'm trans, Paul," she said softly. "I was born male."

"You're trans?" I repeated. "Transgendered?"

"Yes."

I looked straight into her eyes and, crazy as it sounds, I immediately started laughing. I couldn't help myself. Great, giant heaves of laughter poured out of me uncontrollably. I even stood up and started dancing in circles—at least I tried to dance to the best of my ability in the tight confines of the Travato.

"It's not funny, Paul. What are you doing? Are you making fun of me?"

"No, no, no." I quickly ceased my dancing and embraced her instead. "I'm not making fun of you at all. I'm so sorry. I don't mean to diminish what you're saying in the least. I'm just happy, Alex. I'm extremely happy. I thought you were going to say that you had cancer and you were dying."

"Really?" she said, incredulously.

"Of course, really. I don't give a rat's ass about what you were or were not in the past. What I care about is what you are now. If I've learned anything in the last few days, it's that this moment—right here, right now—is all that matters. Whatever got you to this moment, whatever got you to the now, I celebrate *that*, because you are fucking incredible, Alex. Don't you know?"

She let out a slight whimper. "But I should have disclosed it to you from the beginning. That's just common courtesy. It was wrong to dump it on you after the fact."

"I disagree," I said. "Why should you have a higher standard of disclosure than anyone else just because you're trans? You showed me who you are as a person. I liked what I saw, so we had sex. It's that simple. I didn't disclose to you all my baggage, all my history, all my past medical issues. And you didn't expect me to. Why should you have to?"

She looked at me like I was an alien from outer space. "Who the hell are you, Paul? People like you aren't supposed to exist."

"You're saying I should be mad at you because at some point in the past you had a different kind of sexual organ than you do currently, but you didn't tell me? Who cares? It's absurd. Totally absurd. Should you have to tell me every color your hair has ever been too?"

"Hmm, I never thought of it like that. That's pretty well put."

"I'm just sorry you've had to deal with all the stupidity in this society. It's completely unfair and archaic. We're not in the dark ages anymore."

"Okay," she sniffled. "I'm not sure why, but I'm going to let myself believe this is real for a while. Please don't pinch me because I don't want to wake up from this dream... ever."

"I don't want to wake up from it either," I agreed. "Let's stay in it for as long as we can because it's the best dream I've ever had."

Alex sniffled again, but I could tell a huge weight had been lifted from her. "You have yourself a deal, mister," she said, extending her hand. "Because it's the best dream I've ever had too. Thank you, mister nonexistent privileged white male."

"You mean mister nonexistent privileged white *cis* male," I corrected.

"Oh, Master! How could I dare call you, mister? You are totally fucking radically amazing, sir!"

She giggled and threw her arms around me. I twirled her in the air a few times and we both started laughing hysterically. Then I tossed her down on the bed and we proceeded to engage in another round of wild and raucous sex.

TWENTY-TWO

I'll Do It

Later that morning, Bunni knocked on the RV door, inviting us to a poolside brunch. It felt strange to leave our humble lair to enter the sumptuous grounds of Laster's estate, but it felt even stranger to realize that Deliah's funeral had taken place just three days earlier. A twinge of guilt ran through me, as I clasped Alex's hand.

Walking through the garden, I reminded myself that Deliah had divorced me, not the other way around. I'd done everything within my power to make the marriage work. Besides, my bond with Alex was far from a rebound attempt. I had no agenda and I could tell she didn't either.

The dazzling beauty of Point Dume reinforced my desire to remain in the moment. I didn't even flinch when I saw Laster seated next to Bunni at a table overlooking the ocean.

"Good morning, everyone," I said smiling.

"G'murnin," said Alex.

"G'murnin," echoed Bunni.

"What a delight you're joining us," Laster replied. "Please, have a seat."

We shook hands and, as I sat down beside Alex, I felt surprisingly comfortable. I took a long sip of pomegranate juice, then I turned toward Laster and looked into his eyes.

"I really appreciate your overlooking my reckless behavior these past few days, John. You're a better man than I."

"Ah," replied Laster, "but I'm afraid there is no hierarchy in the kingdom of humanity. No hierarchy whatsoever." He took a bite from his acai bowl and passed Alex a platter of raw veggies with fresh hummus.

"No doubt," I continued. "It's just that you've expanded my perception of things. I feel like I'm a little less rigid in my thinking."

"That's wonderful to hear."

"Master often has that effect on people," said Bunni.

"And you enabled me to meet Alex too," I added. "She's amazing." I flashed her a smile and she started to blush.

"Do you think you might be open to further expansion, Paul?" asked Laster.

I paused to scoop up some sprouted lentil dal with a seaweed crisp, as I considered his question. "I believe so, yes," I replied. "What are we here for if not to expand ourselves?"

Both Alex and Bunni chuckled. "So true," said Bunni.

"Good," replied Laster. "I'm having a get-together this afternoon for that express purpose, and I'd very much like it if you and Alex attended."

"A get-together?" I said, glancing sideways at her.

"Perhaps a *trip* would be a better name for it," he clarified.

"What sort of trip?"

"A psychedelic cannabis trip."

"Really? I didn't think cannabis was a hallucinogen."

"You're right. Under ordinary usage, cannabis doesn't alter sensory perceptions the way say, LSD, psilocybin or ayahuasca do."

My head started to spin upon Laster's mentioning of psilocybin. What the hell was he talking about? How dare he mention the substance he'd given Deliah on her last day of life.

"I'm definitely not interested in any of that stuff," I said firmly.

"Of course not," he replied. "You're clearly not a candidate for it, so you're wise to feel that way. But psychedelic cannabis has quite different properties. It's a steady-until-you're-ready kind of trip. While under its influence, you remain in control of the experience and only progress to deeper levels when your nervous system is prepared to handle it."

"Master is an absolute Master when it comes to the art of the trip," enthused Bunni.

He waved his hand dismissively. "I've been fortunate to have access to a great variety of cannabis, thanks to my dispensaries," he said. "The correct mixture is necessary for cannabis to become psychedelic."

"It's all about the blend," added Bunni.

"Bunni is correct. To induce psychedelia, we blend multiple strains of cannabis across the Sativa/Indica spectrum. The secret is to include at least one aged strain as well.

Over time, as cannabis oxidizes and gets exposed to sunlight, its THC converts into cannabinol. The introduction of this cannabinol is what brings the blend into hallucinogenic territory."

"That's all very interesting, but I'm not much of a cannabis user."

"No worries," he said. "You can take as many or as few hits as you want. And if at any time you wish to halt the process, we can administer nano-encapsulated CBD, which will immediately resolve any negative side effects."

I turned to Alex. "Have you done this before?"

"A few times," she replied. "I do think it would be an incredible opportunity for you. It's a powerful medicine."

"A medicine?"

"It releases trauma."

"Hmm," I wavered.

"Do you know how many people would kill to be invited on one of Master's trips?" interjected Bunni. "People fly in from all over the world at a moment's notice for the experience."

"It's just I wasn't expecting..."

Laster stood up from the table. "There will be other opportunities, Paul. If you're not ready, you're not ready."

"Hang on a second," I said, thinking about how brave Alex had been with me.

"Yes?" said Laster expectantly.

"I'll do it," I resolved. "I want to live."

"Aha, that's the spirit."

I squeezed Alex's hand, we all laughed, and the sun scintillated in the sky.

TWENTY-THREE

I Just Was

A GROUP OF THIRTY GUESTS, including Alex and I, occupied the lounge in Laster's mansion. We sat cross-legged on purple mats arranged in a semi-circle. Richly-scented incense wafted through the room and the soft drone of sitar music cast an air of excitement.

The space could have accommodated five times as many people without difficulty, but Laster had kept the invite list to a minimum. Most of the attendees were either VCs, celebrities, crypto investors, or cannabis players.

Somehow, my lack of credentials didn't seem an issue. Three days earlier, I'd raced through this same lounge with two loaded handguns. Now I was contemplating my navel with Alex by my side and billionaires surrounding me. Who ever said life made sense?

Laster and Bunni, adorned in colorful necklaces and scarves, stood on an elevated platform. They were the designated sitters for our journey. If one of us experienced paranoia or a panic attack, their job would be to talk us down and hold our hand.

Far more likely, they assured us, would be positive and transformative feelings such as increased body awareness and a deeper understanding of our purpose. We might even have perceptions of flying or traveling to other dimensions. But I doubted I'd have such sensations, as I'd dabbled with cannabis in college and found it to be largely disappointing.

Most of our preparations focused on breathing—how to engage the belly, how to exhale properly, and how to surrender. Bunni demonstrated various techniques while Laster emphasized the importance of allowing ourselves to feel our bodies and our connection with the earth. Could this be the same couple, I wondered, whose crazed debauchery I'd witnessed earlier?

Before I had time to consider the question, "Eternal Om" began emanating from a massive speaker system. Bunni and Laster handed each of us a water pipe with the psychedelic cannabis blend. Then they assumed the lotus position, fixing their gaze upward until they sensed the moment was right.

"Dear friends gathered here today," Laster began, "let us now call in the sacred plant ally, Cannabis Sativa. Great Healer, we invite you into our bodies, our minds, our spirits, and our hearts. We thank you for making yourself available to each and every one of us. We thank you for this opportunity to share sacred space."

Laster turned slowly to his right side. "Bringing our awareness to the east, we call upon the spirit of new beginnings and clear vision. With ever-present gratitude and humility, we take this venerated medicine." He drew a long puff from his pipe and motioned for us to do likewise if we felt so inclined.

After his tribute to the east, he proceeded to make similar invocations to the other directions: south, west, north, below, above, and within. Each time, he adjusted his bearing accordingly, offered a heartfelt word of thanks, and took a puff from his pipe. I followed his lead without difficulty, as the blend tasted quite smooth and flavorful.

The music transitioned to "Crystal Bowls Chakra Chants" and we were given an opportunity to ingest further medicine. I inhaled two more hits from my pipe, enticed by the way the smoke felt as it entered my lungs. Then we all lay on our backs and placed masks over our eyes.

"Weightless" started playing through the speakers, as Laster eased us into a body scan meditation. He walked us through the process of tracking what we were most aware of in our bodies, watching where this awareness moved and breathing fully as we did. When we encountered resistance or tension, he invited us to visualize it slowly dissipating, like the melting of ice in a glacier field.

I took to the meditation with surprising ease and fluidity. Whenever I detected an area in my body of significant tension, I envisioned releasing it like removing plaque when flossing my teeth. Steadily and methodically, I let go of the buildup in my arms, legs, neck, face, and upper body.

As I did, my perception of the space within me grew larger and more expansive. A universe unto itself opened before me with endless time to explore it. I could do this forever, I realized. I felt so peaceful, so free, so calm. There was no need to be anywhere else. No need to do anything else. Releasing, releasing, releasing. Breathing, breathing, breathing.

When I arrived at my pelvic region, the space within me quickly contracted. Everything turned to white light. It wasn't frightening or oppressive, but I felt like I lost control of my sensory apparatus and I couldn't detect the music or Laster's voice anymore. Instead, I heard Deliah talking. Her face seemed like it was inches from my own, but it didn't have any trace of that sad look to which I was accustomed.

"You're doing great!" she exclaimed. "I'm so proud of you, Paul!

"Deliah?" I tried to speak her name, but no sound issued from my lips.

"It's okay," she said. "Don't talk. Whatever you want to tell me, just think it. I can read your mind."

"Please forgive me, Deliah." This was my primary thought, my biggest concern.

"For what?"

"For Alex. Did I hurt your feelings? Are you mad at me for finding her?"

"Don't be silly, Paul! I'm happy you're with Alex! I love both of you!"

"You do?"

"Of course I do! She's amazing and so are you!"

"You don't mind that it all happened so quickly?"

"Just the opposite. I'm glad about it."

"Really?"

"It's all I've ever wanted for you—to feel loved and accepted."

"I never knew you cared about that."

"I know. I'm sorry I didn't ever tell you. You deserve it, Paul."

"But why couldn't *you* love me that way?"

"I wanted to. I really, really wanted to. Please know that."

"Then why did you leave me? I've missed you so much, Deliah."

"Oh, Paul. I didn't leave you. I'm right here. I'll always be here for you."

"No, no, it's not true." I started to twist and flail. "You're gone. This isn't reality."

"It *is* reality. I'm still here. I'm going to prove it to you. You'll see."

"How? How? How are you going to prove it?"

"I love you, Paul."

Her face vanished as quickly as it had appeared. And now I was floating. Floating in the white light. No breathing and releasing. No twisting and flailing. Just floating, floating, floating in a never-ending expanse of pure white light.

I still wasn't frightened. I wasn't even sad or agitated. I just was. I just was what was.

TWENTY-FOUR

The Third Thing

WHEN I REMOVED my eye mask, I saw that everyone had left the lounge except for Alex. Her legs were cradled around my torso with my head resting on her belly. I enjoyed the warmth of her body for a moment, then I slowly lifted myself up to a seated position.

"How are you?" asked Alex. "Is everything okay?"

"I'm fine, I'm good." I turned and gave her a kiss. "I missed you though. How long have I been in this state?"

"About four hours. Everyone else left a while ago. You must have gone really deep. You were totally out of it."

"It was pretty intense," I said.

"Do you want to take a walk and share our experiences?" she asked.

I agreed and we headed for the shoreline. We walked leisurely, hand-in-hand, enjoying the coastal beauty of the early evening. Everything felt easy and unlabored—the opposite of how most of my life had been—and I realized I was still high from the cannabis.

As we stopped to dip our toes in the water, I told Alex how grateful I was that she'd stayed by my side in the lounge. She looked at me like it was nothing, surprised that I'd even mentioned the subject. I hugged her and began recounting my success with releasing tension from my body.

She told me the session had been rewarding for her too. Not only had she loosened some stubborn trigger points in her abdomen, but she'd managed to let go of a big chunk of her unresolved anger toward her father. He'd never even acknowledged her transition and still referred to her as a male.

I gave her another long embrace, this time with a french kiss. The sun was setting and we decided to continue strolling eastward past Paradise Cove. I kept thinking how incredible it felt to be with her. It seemed impossible that such a simple thing could feel that good.

As the last rays of light struck the beach, my eye caught the sun's reflection in a window—it was from the bungalow where I'd found Deliah. The memory didn't stab me in the gut like I expected it would. Instead, I dug my hand into a pocket of my jeans and fished out the key Laster had given me.

"Do you want to go in?" I asked, casting my gaze toward the guest house.

"Only if you do," said Alex. "It's up to you, Master."

"Let's take a quick look."

We trudged up the trail, still hand-in-hand. I suppose it was a test of sorts. I felt so good, I wanted to know if the sensation would endure, even if I stretched myself to face something uncomfortable.

"Stick in hole, push," I said, as I inserted the key into the deadbolt and opened the front door.

"Oh, Master," she replied smiling, "stick in hole, push."

To my surprise, the bungalow had been cleaned up and was immaculate. Not a shred of evidence of Deliah's demise remained. New paint, rugs, furniture, appliances, and artwork had been added to spruce up the place and the kitchen was fully stocked with high-end food from Erewhon.

"Did John do all this?" I asked.

"I think Bunni said she did it. She used to be an interior designer."

"Impressive."

"It's much nicer than I expected," agreed Alex. "It's my first time seeing it."

"Really? I thought you might have hung out here with Deliah."

"Actually, I never met her. I wish I had." She looked at me nervously. "Is that weird for me to say?"

"Not in the least. You two would have hit it off, I'm sure. But I'm a bit confused. Didn't she spend time at the house when she was with John?"

"Not that I ever saw. I've only been there for the past couple of weeks, so I don't know the whole history. It was Deliah who recommended me to John though. Apparently, she saw me dancing at the CuntGrind."

"Oh," I said nonchalantly. "I guess I don't understand how these things work. So... am I interfering in any way with your duties to him?"

"No, silly," she gasped. "I'm not his employee. I'm his guest."

"Sorry, I don't mean to pry. Being in here is making me feel a bit off-kilter."

She reached to stroke my hair. "Of course, that makes total sense. Do you want to leave?"

"I sort of do, but I sort of want to eat some of this amazing food too."

"Oh, god, I'm so glad you said that. I'm starving."

"So am I."

"Why don't you relax on the couch, Master, and I'll whip up an incredible meal for us."

"Me likes that idea."

We both laughed and she set about preparing dinner. I took her suggestion and reclined on a plush couch while enjoying a panoramic view of orange, magenta, and purple clouds hovering over the Pacific. I was still feeling reasonably good, considering the circumstances.

Seeing Deliah's MacBook on the coffee table, I decided it was finally time to check out painsluts.com. That would be the true test. Could I look at her videos without losing my composure?

I opened Safari, typed in the domain name, and the homepage loaded instantly. It featured an image of three big-breasted females pounding each other's holes using strap-on dildos thicker than baseball bats, while a man with gargantuan pecs rammed his horse-like cock into one of the female's throats. Pretty commonplace stuff.

At the top right corner of the site, I saw I'd been automatically logged into Deliah's account. Her username appeared in bold red: PsycheDeliah. I clicked on it and was taken to a page that showed the videos in which she was featured, as well as her profile details.

Of the twenty-three videos listed, every single one of them involved anal sex. The vast majority of them were lesbian-themed. They featured titles like *PsycheDeliah Loves Ass Gapes*, *Double Anal Fisting for PsycheDeliah*, and *PsycheDeliah's Lesbian Prolapse Party*.

I muted the sound on the laptop and began randomly watching scenes. The whole time, I squinted my eyes. As I viewed the flickering light on the screen, I imagined I was an alien from another planet studying human beings for the first time.

Sometimes, the human beings took off their clothes in order to rub their nipples, skin, and genitalia against each other. Sometimes, they explored each other's orifices using fingers, tongues, dildos, or other objects. Sometimes, the explorations produced pleasure—sometimes pain.

And how did it all matter? Was it significant that these humans seemed most attracted to anal orifices? Was there a reason they sought to fill and stretch their cavities to seemingly impossible extents? Were they trying to overcome something by inducing such pain?

I froze up with the last question because, in some remote crevice of my brain, I knew the answer—and not as an alien, but as myself. Which meant it was no longer possible to play the game of pretending to be an alien. Which meant it was no longer possible to feel good. Which meant I wasn't high anymore.

Just as I stopped the squinting exercise, Alex arrived with steaming plates for each of us. I closed the laptop and gestured for her to sit next to me on the couch. We were both so hungry, we only paused to clink our wine glasses before devouring our meal of wild grilled salmon with Japanese sweet potatoes and broccolini.

When we were sufficiently sated, Alex inquired about what I'd been doing on the laptop. I decided, rather dramatically, to show her the screen instead of replying with words. I lifted up the lid and, as it so happened, the last video I'd been watching was paused on a gynecological close-up of Deliah being fucked in the ass by a woman wielding a strap-on dildo.

"Wow!" she exclaimed. "Do you want to try that on me?"

I looked up at her, speechless.

"I'm sorry. Did I say something wrong?"

"No... no," I stammered. "It's... it's just that seeing that image made me realize two things that I desperately need to tell you. Well, three things actually."

"Three things? All from that?"

"Yes, exactly."

"That's so weird."

"Why? What do you mean?"

"Because now that I'm looking at the image, I'm realizing I have three things I desperately need to tell you too."

"Woah," I said.

"So who's going first?"

"Can we do it together?"

"I don't see why not."

"Okay," I said slowly. "Here goes number one."

"Number one."

"I love you, Alex," I blurted out.

Her eyes widened and I knew it was the same for her.

"I love you, Paul," she echoed.

The exchange was effortless, selfless, and pure—unlike

any other love proclamation I'd ever made. I reached for her hand, holding it tight, and we kissed softly. We kissed so softly it felt deeper than a deep kiss, and I felt courage welling up inside of me.

"Thing number two now?" I asked. "Even though it's a bit harder?"

"Yes, thing number two," she agreed. "And yeah, I know what you mean."

I took a deep breath and let it out without further consideration. "When I was an eight-year-old boy, I was anally raped. Repeatedly. Over and over."

Alex quivered and her eyes became moist. "Sweet Master, I knew you were going to say that. When I was an eight-year-old boy, I was anally raped too. Repeatedly. Over and over."

"Oh... oh," I faltered, "I didn't know you were going to say that."

"It's okay," she said, reaching to hold me tight. "It's okay. I'm so glad you told me. So, so glad."

"Me too. It's strange that we have that in common and yet it makes so much sense."

"Exactly. It's strange and comforting at the same time."

"You're right."

We hugged each other on the couch for several minutes —rocking each other, stroking each other, and soothing each other. Gradually, the night sky set in around us, the wind began to intensify, and the light from the full moon crept into the living room.

There were so many questions for us to consider and so many answers too. But it was our wondering about the third thing that made its way to the forefront of our minds.

"Are you ready for the last one now?" I said.

"Yes," she replied, "the third thing."

"Together?"

"Together."

"*That*," we said simultaneously, pointing at the image on the laptop screen and both smiling devilishly.

And what we meant, of course, was that I wanted to try anal on her as much as she wanted me to try it on her.

Even though. Yes.

And because of. Yes.

And for the obvious reason too. Yes.

Not One More Day

For the next couple of hours, Alex and I sat on the couch talking, hugging, laughing, and crying. There was a lot to process and, while we were relieved to have named our childhood traumas, neither one of us was eager to delve into too many specifics. Instead, we celebrated their commonality and focused on how our experiences had brought us closer together.

We even watched more videos on painsluts.com, although we deliberately avoided the ones that featured Deliah. It was the first time I'd felt so safe and comfortable in the realm of sexuality. We were free to be exactly who we were, without fear of censure or judgment.

Alex grew so relaxed, she fell into a deep sleep on my shoulder. I didn't have the heart to wake her, as much as I'd been looking forward to getting naked with her. The downtime gave me an opportunity to try to make sense of what I'd learned about Deliah.

On one level, I felt saddened that she'd been so drawn to

anal sex. She'd performed in at least twenty-three hardcore videos featuring the act, all secretly, all while still married to me. Clearly, I'd failed to meet her needs for a long time. Perhaps worse, I'd been an embarrassingly unobservant husband to have not noticed her steady stream of side gigs.

On another level though, I felt liberated by the discovery, even comforted. At last, I had some sort of explanation, if only partial, for why my marriage had failed. And although some people might say an attraction to anal sex was shallow and immature, even perverse, I knew in the deepest recesses of my being that it most certainly was not.

Admittedly, Deliah and I had been disappointed by our experiences with Tantra, but we'd both agreed the principles were sound. As any number of studies showed, sexuality between consenting adults could be a profound vehicle for overcoming trauma. Because of the high concentration of nerve endings surrounding the anus and perineum, anal sex offered the potential for greater healing than any of the other erogenous zones.

But even though I knew this, I'd remained closed-minded about it. Deliah had invited me to try anal with her countless times and I'd spurned her on each and every occasion. I'd never yielded to her wishes even once—what normal man would do that? Several of my previous girlfriends had wanted it too, but I'd always found a way to put them off without giving a good reason, and certainly not the real reason.

In high school, I once got invited to a "slumber party" with three of the most popular girls in school—and no other guys. It wasn't because I was anybody special, per se, but because I happened to look like the most sought-after boy in town, the star quarterback on the football team who had the coolest clothes, the fastest car, and the wealthiest parents. By association, I became the number two catch until I destroyed my reputation.

The fiasco started like a page from *Penthouse Forum*. Jenny, a raven-haired tigress, approached me one afternoon while I was playing a pick-up game of volleyball. She pulled me off the court, planted a kiss on my lips, and told me she had a huge crush on me.

While spoon-feeding me frozen yogurt, she whispered in my ear her biggest fantasy—to have me to herself in her house to do all the naughty things she'd been imagining. The only reason she hadn't told me about her crush sooner, she sighed, was because her parents never went anywhere.

But the parents of her best friend, Julie, were going out of town that very night, she explained excitedly. Julie had no siblings, no housekeepers, no relatives that might show up unannounced. The entire house would be empty—except for her other best friend, Jessica, whom she'd also invited.

Running her hands across my chest, she asked if I'd like to make her fantasy come true. To help me decide, she let me know that both Julie and Jessica had mini-crushes on me too. I pretended I was used to getting such invitations, telling her I had to check my calendar, but inside I was quavering with excitement.

The evening started off in textbook fashion with the four of us hanging out by the pool. We drank beer, threw back Jell-O shots, and played games like spin the bottle and strip poker—all the usual stuff horny teenagers do. I kept telling myself it was no big deal, just another typical evening lounging with three super-sexy females who dug me.

I seemed to be pulling off the charade reasonably well too. Halfway into the evening, I was the only one left wearing any articles of clothing. When Jenny suggested we get into the hot tub, I quickly peeled off my briefs and led my naked admirers into the bubbly, frothing water.

With the three J's bouncing and jiggling around me, there was little doubt where things would head. Nature took its expected course. In no time, I was licking their nipples, rubbing their pussies, and getting my dick and balls sucked like they were the most prized jewels in the world.

Primed from the foreplay, Jenny soon seized the moment and guided my cock into her slippery wet pussy. I fucked her like a wild stallion, while Julie and Jessica cheered us on. Once Jenny was suitably spent, she passed me off to Julie and Jessica. Then we repeated the cycle all over again.

Pulling my cock out of one eager pussy, pushing it into another, back and forth, again and again, over and over, I knew I was experiencing a dream-come-true that would last my entire lifetime. The girls were loving it. I was loving it. It was beyond insane.

Until the curveball came. From out of nowhere, Jenny suggested I fuck her ass instead of her pussy. The other girls all cooed and squealed in excitement. They were absolutely on fire with lust and desire.

"Do it, Paul!" exclaimed Julie.

"Fuck her in the ass!" cried Jessica.

"Please, fuck my ass!" begged Jenny.

"After you fuck her ass, fuck mine!"

"And then fuck mine!"

"Fuck all of our assholes, Paul!"

"We want you, Paul!"

"We need you, Paul!"

Contrary to what an expert in human sexuality might predict, my cock did not respond to their beseeching comments by getting harder. Rather, it went limp and shriveled to total nothingness. Flaccid is the technical term, I believe.

I had no idea what to say. My mind went completely blank. I couldn't think of a single explanation, a single action to take, that would right the situation. How could I possibly fix this? It was beyond humiliating, beyond emasculating.

All I could do was lift myself out of the hot tub, grab my clothes, and run. Run, run, run all the way back to my bedroom. Climb in through the window and bury myself under the sheets. And hope, hope, hope beyond hope that everything would be forgotten the next day.

But of course, it wasn't. When I arrived at school, the first thing I saw painted in bold red letters all over the wall of lockers next to my homeroom was: "WOLNIAK IS A PRUDE!"

Among my peers anyway, no word in the English language had the ability to ruin one's reputation more thoroughly and completely than *prude*. Serial killer would have been better—a lot better. I might as well have been a cockroach, as far as everyone else was concerned, because I had officially become undatable, unfriendable, unfuckable. For all intents and purposes, it was the end of Paul Wolniak in my small town.

After I graduated high school and left Dodge, I got over it—for the most part. But what I didn't get over was the root issue. Why was I so intensely bent out of shape by the prospect of anal sex? Why, why, why?

Not until my psychedelic cannabis session, over a decade later, could I see that the answer was ridiculously simple. It was just a matter of facing the truth I'd been avoiding, the truth about what had happened to me as a boy.

Before using Laster's blend, when memories of my childhood trauma flickered across my mind, I immediately suppressed them. Or if I somehow failed to shunt them into the background, then I beat myself up, telling myself it must have been my fault because of some defect I had or because I wanted attention of some sort. I certainly never accepted the truth plainly and simply— that I was an innocent eight-year-old boy who was anally raped by a sadistic pedophile.

Once I was honest with myself about it, once I dared to state it that directly, the answer became obvious. I didn't want to have anal sex because I didn't want to be reminded of being raped. It had hurt like hell and made me feel like a worthless piece of shit. Who wants to be reminded of that?

There was another factor too. Not just one perpetrator had been involved in my molestation. There'd been two adults, two adult males, so-called friends of my father and supposed pillars of the community. One was the dean of the college and the other the provost. They'd each taken turns raping me and they didn't just do it once, but multiple times.

When I thought about it more, there was a third factor too. My father had invited these two rapists into our house. They were regular guests at the cocktail mixers he hosted every few months, as chairman of the sociology department.

On one such evening, he uncharacteristically checked in on me, poking his head in my bedroom to make sure I was asleep. That was when he saw the dean raping me in the ass while the provost pinned me down on my bed. My mouth was gagged with a hand towel, but I managed to catch my father's eyes for a moment. He just turned around in his tracks and shut the door behind him—never saying a word about the matter to me, nor disinviting the two rapists to his subsequent parties.

All these factors taken together seemed like a pretty decent explanation for my aversion to anal sex. And it actually felt good to recount them to myself, to name them and feel their weight and give them their due recognition. Because they made me appreciate that I wasn't nearly as fucked up as I always thought I was.

In fact, for the first time, I realized that Deliah would have surely forgiven me for ignoring her needs—if only I'd told her about what had happened. It was a hard pill to swallow because our whole marriage would have been different if I'd been able to do that. But I felt certain she would have forgiven me for my silence too. She even would have understood why I now wanted to have anal sex with Alex.

I vowed to myself then that the cycle of abuse was officially over. Not one more day was going to pass with this motherfucking noose around my neck. Not a single one. Because I was sick of being ruled by my past. And I was sick of letting my father's neglect and his two rapist friends dictate my entire life.

Of all the people who'd ever walked the earth, Deliah would have understood that better than anyone.

TWENTY-SIX

Completely F'd Up

We spent the night in the bungalow—in the same bedroom where I'd found Deliah's naked body. Since Alex never woke up from her slumber, I carried her there from the couch. The room had been redecorated with new furniture and accessories, making it quite comfortable.

I slept deeply, despite the bungalow's troubled history. Being in the same space where Deliah spent her final hours didn't bother me, perhaps because of my recent realizations —and the cannabis in my bloodstream. The outside forces that had once separated us now seemed to be bringing us back together.

When I woke up the next morning, Alex was tenderly fellating me. I offered to reciprocate, but she insisted that I lay still and let her service me. As before, she took her time, building my desire in waves, then backing off and repeating.

With some practice, I found I could relax instead of tensing, even as I approached my edge. I imagined myself floating in a warm pool of seawater on a Hawaiian island. It struck me as almost humorous that I had to train myself to receive pleasure in the copious amounts Alex provided.

After almost an hour with my cock fully engorged, I reached my limit and knew I could tolerate no more—not even for one second. In a frenzied swoop, I lifted Alex up and planted her on all fours. Then I started fucking her pussy from behind.

"Master!" she moaned. "Aren't you forgetting something?"

"How much I love you?"

"Not that, Master," she giggled. "The third thing."

"Oh... *that*."

A part of me recoiled at the reference, but a bigger part felt excitement. I reminded myself that I wasn't an eight-year-old boy anymore. I was safe. Everything was okay.

"I'm ready," she said coyly, raising her backside.

I withdrew my cock and ran my hands across her cheeks, letting my saliva drip down her crack. She gasped in delight and further arched her back. I responded by teasing the rim of her asshole.

"Master! You're so good at this!"

Using my free hand, I began gently touching her outer labia. I parted her moist lips like the petals of a flower and, ever so slightly, I pushed a finger inside her pussy. I slid the finger downwards until it touched her clit. Alex gasped more loudly.

"Please fuck my ass! Please, Master!"

The sound of her begging made my confidence grow. I rubbed her clit harder and pushed my index finger inside her ass, just a quarter-inch or so. Then I quickly pulled it out, teased the rim again, and dripped more saliva into her hole.

"Master, it feels so good! I need you to fuck my ass with your cock!"

I plunged my finger inside her more deeply and immediately pulled it back out.

"Please, Master! I beg you! Please put your cock in my ass!"

My intention was to continue the foreplay for a while longer, but her entreaties made it impossible. I had to give her what she wanted. My own wishes were irrelevant, as were my hang-ups. The here and now was all that mattered.

"Take it, slut!" I declared. And without further delay, I nudged the tip of my hard cock into her wet, throbbing hole.

"More, Master! Please! I need more!"

I retracted the tip and swiftly pushed it back in.

"I love your hard cock, Master!"

"Are you sure?"

"Yes, Master! Give me more, pleeeeeeeeease!"

I continued teasing her ass with the tip, in and out, in and out, each time parting her ass cheeks a bit wider and filling her hole a bit deeper.

"Ooooh, it feels so good, Master!"

"Does the slut need more?" I asked, lightly smacking her protruding orbs.

"Oh, yes, Master!" she cried. "Yes!"

I spanked her again and suddenly slid my cock halfway inside her. The sensation exceeded all of my expectations. How could such pleasure be possible? I felt so free, so unencumbered like I was floating on clouds. My entire being tingled from head to toe.

"Master, this is amazing! You're amazing!"

I kept pumping her ass, each time pushing a little further, a little harder, until my balls were slapping against her cheeks. Alex met my strokes perfectly with her own undulations, allowing my cock to probe still deeper. Together, we moaned and groaned, thrust and lunged, in a rhythmic dance of lust and desire.

I lost track of all sense of time and place as we became engulfed in cosmic bliss. Everything was here. This was what I'd always needed, what I'd been lacking my entire life. How had I lived for twenty-nine years without experiencing such ecstasy and fulfillment?

"Master, I'm cumming!" cried Alex. "Cum with me, Master! Please, cum with me!"

She bucked and screeched wildly, her red hair flying everywhere, and she began to orgasm in great arcing waves. The sight was so beautiful to witness, I had no hope of holding back any longer. All the accumulated pain and sorrow of my life evaporated in an instant, like a flash of lightning, as I watched Alex's angelic face express her pleasure.

I realized then I was orgasming too, but the release was far more intense than any prior one—it might as well have been my first time. Merged with the wondrous eternal, I pounded Alex's ass one last time and exploded inside of her. My movement was so vigorous, so unbridled, I inadvertently caused the bed mattress to slide off its frame.

Together, we went tumbling onto the floor, knocking over the nightstand. A lamp and an iPad landed inches from Alex's head. We both burst into laughter, a tangled sticky mess of passion and joy.

"Oh, Master, that was incredible!" exclaimed Alex.

"You were incredible!" I replied. "You were beyond incredible!"

I shifted my position and began spooning her from behind, as we basked in the feeling of true love. We lay in this manner for some time, until I noticed Alex studying the back of the iPad. It was resting in front of her face and I could tell something about it had captured her attention.

"What?" I said. "What is it?"

"The engraving on the iPad. It says *Deliah Olaffson*."

"Olaffson was her maiden name," I explained. "She never took my last name."

Alex sat up and looked at me, her face turning white. "That's... that's not possible," she stuttered.

"What do you mean?" I asked.

"Deliah Olaffson was my best friend as a kid."

"Huh?"

"We played together all the time when I was a little boy."

"I'm totally confused, Alex. Where did you grow up?"

"Palo Alto."

"Come on," I replied sternly. "That's not funny. Palo Alto is where Deliah grew up."

"I know, Paul. We grew up together. Her parents were Walter and Iolana."

Now I began turning white. "Is this some kind of game you're playing?"

Alex shook her head. "I'm telling you the truth."

"But how could you only be realizing this now?" I barked. "You've known her first name was Deliah all this time. It's not that common of a name."

"You think I'm covering something up? You think I have some ulterior motive?"

"Of course not," I said softly, realizing I'd overstepped.

"It never occurred to me until now that they could be one and the same person," she insisted. "Not once."

"I'm sorry. I'm just confused and shocked. I don't understand what's going on."

"Well, I don't either."

"Please forgive me, Alex," I said, holding out my hands to embrace her. "I'm really sorry for doubting you."

"It's okay," she sighed. "I shouldn't be so defensive. I can see why you'd be confused." She let out an even bigger sigh. "There's some stuff I haven't told you, Paul. It's probably why I didn't make the connection sooner."

"What kind of stuff?"

She paused for a moment, her eyes moistening. "This is hard for me."

"You can tell me anything. I promise." I reached out to stroke her hair.

"You remember about me being raped when I was eight?"

"Absolutely. I'll never forget."

"It was Walter who did it. Walter Olaffson was the man who raped me in the ass—repeatedly."

"What?" I bolted up from the floor and began gesticulating. "What the fuck? I'll kill that motherfucker!"

"Paul, let me finish."

"There's no fucking way! I can't take this! It's too much! It's too fucking much!"

"Please, just hear me out. I need to get this off my chest."

I was foaming at the mouth, barely able to breathe. It seemed impossible that I had just enjoyed the most amazing love-making of my life and now suddenly this shit was happening. How could the universe be so cruel? It took every ounce of discipline I had in order to remain still enough to listen to what Alex had to say.

"Even as a young boy," she continued, "even when I was just four or five, I always identified with my feminine side. Deliah was cool with it, which was why I hung out with her so much. She didn't look at me as male or female. Just as a kid."

I nodded my head. "Yeah, I can see her being like that."

"At home, I wasn't able to express that side of myself at all. Not even in the slightest way. My parents were too freaked out by it. So I must have overcompensated or something when I was at Deliah's house and that's how I got into trouble. Without meaning to excite him, I guess I sort of flirted with Walter. He would start to show interest in me when I acted girlishly and, I have to admit, it kind of excited me. I guess I encouraged it in a way over the years. But I never, never, never wanted to be raped. I was just a little kid. I just wanted some attention to make up for what I wasn't getting at home. That was it." Alex began sobbing.

"First of all," I replied, "I believe you one hundred percent, so you don't need to worry about that at all."

"Thank you," she whimpered.

"Secondly, no, you didn't overcompensate. You didn't do anything wrong whatsoever. You were just experimenting to figure out who you were. Only a complete psychopath would exploit an innocent child in the state you were in. It doesn't matter whether you were flirting or not, okay? You were just a kid. It's never, never, never acceptable or forgivable for an adult to do what Walter did."

"You're sure?"

"Beyond sure. Yes. He's an absolute criminal."

She took a big breath. "I think that might be why I didn't put it together when I heard Deliah's name after coming to live at John's house. I'd blocked out that whole episode of my childhood and never told anyone what had happened. Not even my parents. After Walter did what he did to me, I stopped going to Deliah's house. I dropped her completely as a friend and I never explained anything to her. It was awful of me."

"That wasn't awful of you. It was completely understandable, given the circumstances. How could you have been expected to know what to do in a situation like that?"

"You really think so?"

"I do. Completely."

"So you see now why I didn't even consider the possibility that she could be the same Deliah I knew as I kid? It was just too loaded of a thing from my past for my brain to go there."

"Yes, I understand. It makes perfect sense."

"And keep in mind, she didn't have blonde hair then—it was jet black when I knew her. When she was a kid, she didn't look anything like she did in those painslut videos."

"I get it, I totally get it."

"Really?"

I gave her a big hug. "Yes, really. I do."

"So we're good?"

"Yes, we're good, Alex. But I have to be honest with you. I'm *not* good. I'm completely fucked up. And now I need your help."

"How? Anything?"

"I need you to let me go do what I have to do."

"What are you saying?"

"Please. I have to go. Right now."

"Then I'm coming with you, Paul."

"No, I need you to stay here. I'm sorry. I love you, but I have to do this on my own."

I kissed her on the lips, threw on some clothes, and charged out of the bungalow. Alex followed after me onto the beach, but I was a strong runner and she didn't stand a chance. By the time I passed the pier at Paradise Cove, I was already a hundred yards ahead of her.

TWENTY-SEVEN

Swan Dive

In a matter of minutes, I reached Laster's estate. Fortunately, Bunni had given me the access code for the fourth bay of the garage, where both the Mercedes and the Travato were stowed. I input the code and the door swiftly retracted.

The problem was remembering where I'd put the key fob for the roadster. It wasn't in the vehicle—that was the first place I checked. Frantically, I searched all the counters, shelves, and drawers in the RV, as well as the pockets of my dirty trousers. Nothing.

I considered firing up the Travato, as that key was lying on the dashboard, but I needed speed. Besides, the roadster was in the front of the bay, so there was no way to get the Travato out of the garage unless the roadster was moved—and there was no way to move the roadster without its key fob.

"Fuck!" I screamed. "Fuck! Fuck! Fuck!"

"Is everything okay?" asked Bunni, peering into the bay.

"Sorry, I didn't know you were here."

"I saw you running up the trail. I thought maybe you needed help."

"What I need is the damn key to the roadster. I've got to get out of here."

"Is that the key?" she asked, pointing to a fob dangling from a hook on the wall.

"Oh god, yes," I replied. I snatched it and leaped into the roadster, worried that Alex might be getting close.

"Is there anything else you need? John is home today and I'm sure he'd love to help."

"Not where I'm going, I'm afraid."

"Where's that?"

"To war, Bunni. I'm going to war."

"War? That doesn't sound good."

"Tell John I love him, okay?" I revved the engine and began backing out of the garage.

"Uh, okay."

"If I return, I'll be his student for life. And if I don't, give all my possessions to Alex."

"Of course, but..."

"I love you too, Bunni."

Before she had a chance to reply, I peeled out of the driveway leaving a trail of burnt rubber. I didn't even check for oncoming traffic. My heart was beating like a drum.

When I reached the first traffic light, I came to a full stop and took a deep breath. Enough people had already been hurt, I told myself. This was not the time to behave recklessly and risk more people's safety.

I looked over my shoulder to confirm I wasn't being

followed. Then I calmly veered northward on the PCH. I decided I'd take Highway 101 this time, as I definitely wasn't in the mood for the central valley.

The stop-and-go traffic didn't thin out until I reached Zuma. There I accelerated to sixty-five miles per hour and maintained it all the way to Point Mugu. I intended to drive safely, yes, but I sure as hell wasn't going to obey the posted limits.

In Oxnard, I picked up the 101 and increased my cruising speed to eighty-five. The mellow tone of the exhaust let me know that the GT R was unchallenged by my sedate driving, but I stayed the course. Another hour or two wouldn't make much difference in the greater scheme of things.

As I drove, I kept visualizing Alex at age eight being raped by Walter. On the one hand, it seemed inconceivable that a lanky Swedish engineer wearing a pocket protector could be capable of such a hideous act. On the other hand, the moment Alex shared her secret, I knew it was true.

Maybe it was because I'd suffered the same violation at the same age. Maybe it was because I loved and trusted Alex. Or maybe it was because I'd witnessed a narcissism in Walter's comments that suggested a hidden, darker side. All I knew was that I'd seen the absolute veracity of Alex's claim in her eyes.

Worse yet, I felt sure it wasn't the only act of rape Walter had committed. From the moment Alex outed him, I could smell his trail of abuse. How many victims he'd terrorized was anyone's guess. The question was what to do about it. I only had a few more hours to come up with a strategy.

In the meantime, I wept. At first, only a few small tears

dripped out of the corner of my eyes. I dried them with my hands and sniffled them away.

But even as I focused my attention on the cars ahead of me and thought about mundane matters, the tears kept coming. It soon became apparent I couldn't suppress them. As they grew, wails of grief began pouring out of me—heaving, moaning wails, each one greater than the previous.

I'd had a few big sobs in my lifetime—the divorce and Deliah's death certainly incited them. But nothing had ever hit me this hard. I sounded like a rabid coyote alternating between fits of howling, blubbering, and whimpering. Anyone passing me by on the highway would have surely thought I was a mad man.

It was as if Alex's revelation allowed me to finally feel my own molestation. I'd been too young to process it when it happened—an eight-year-old has no frame of reference. But as an adult, the outrageous injustice of Alex's rape was easy to recognize, which put me in touch with the injustice of mine.

I yielded to the catharsis so deeply that I barely seemed to occupy the roadster as I traveled northward. Hours passed without my absorbing the scenery around me. I just kept crying and purging, weeping and releasing. It wasn't until I reached San Luis Obispo and saw the turn-off for Route 1 that my perceptual apparatus reengaged.

I realized then I had to go through Big Sur again. I needed to guide the roadster through the wind-swept, mist-laden mountains one more time. But I needed to make the journey as a whole man, as a man who'd faced his demons and come out on the other side.

As I took the exit for Morro Bay, I retracted the convertible top. It was time to leave the shadow of my cocoon and enter into the sunlight. It was time to do battle, to fight for what was right, under the protection of the Solarbeam Yellow.

Approaching the deep blue Pacific, I dialed Maher's number. I didn't expect the jerk to pick up. I didn't expect anything, but he was the only lawyer I knew, so I figured it was a reasonable starting place.

"Law Offices," he said.

"Gene?" I replied. "You're answering your own phones now?"

He bellowed like I'd just told him the funniest joke ever. "Pauly, buddy! What's up?"

"Quick question. Do you know the statute of limitations for rape, sodomy, and sexual abuse of a minor?"

"Criminal or civil?"

"Whatever causes the most damage for the perp."

"Gotcha. Well, in California there's no longer a statute of limitations for the criminal charges. But for civil, a child rape victim has until age twenty-six to file a claim."

"Very interesting," I said.

"What's this all about, Pauly?"

"Nothing I'm able to discuss right now. But I'll let you know if and when that changes."

"Please do. I have an associate who crushes when it comes to rape prosecution."

"Good to know. Good to know."

"Everything else okay?" he asked.

"Yeah, everything's great," I said, noticing a car on my tail. "I gotta go, Gene. Talk later."

"Later, Pauly."

A red Tesla roadster was following about fifty yards behind me—it'd been weaving through traffic for the past few minutes. I'd never seen one in the wild before, as they hadn't been officially released yet, but I knew a bit about them because one of my office mates at MediaCow had put down a deposit. The claim was they could do zero to sixty in 1.9 seconds and hit a top speed in excess of two fifty. In other words, they could smoke my GT R.

I purposely slowed down and the Tesla adjusted its speed accordingly. I sped up and ditto. Whoever this joker was, he didn't seem very good at concealing himself.

Fuck it, I sort of liked the idea of a suitor. I decided to play it cool. Why show my cards upfront? I might as well let the Tesla make the first move.

I drove at a steady fifty miles per hour past Cayucos, Cambria, and the Hearst Castle. I didn't so much as glance in the rear-view mirror. I just minded my own business and twiddled my thumbs, okey-dokey. No one passed me and I didn't pass anyone.

It wasn't until I came to the first hairpin turn at Ragged Point that my impatience got the better of me. If the Tesla wasn't going to do a damn thing, I would. I jammed the shifter into second and slammed the pedal to the floor. Cowabunga. The GT R roared like a lion and I was officially out of there.

I shifted into third on the straightaway and kept the pedal to the metal. As the speedometer crossed a hundred, I let out a bellicose laugh—until I checked my mirror. What the hell? The Tesla was still on my ass.

I backed down to fifty, but the red irritant refused to do anything besides ride me. I dropped my speed all the way to thirty and held it for five solid minutes. Same thing.

Now I was getting mad. It was time to drive hard and do what I came here to do. I dropped into second again and floored it. Once I redlined, I shifted into third and continued holding down the pedal until I hit one twenty. The Tesla remained glued to my ass.

One twenty into the curves was pretty dang challenging, but I'd done it before, so I knew I could do it again. Whoosh. The GT R barely seemed to strain. I, on other hand, was blown out of my mind—with the top down, the sensation was unlike anything I'd ever experienced. Why had I waited this long?

I glanced in the mirror and, to my shock and amazement, my tail was lagging. Holy shit, the Tesla might have the speed advantage, but my poor old AMG GT R still had some performance chops. I let out a war cry and gave the finger to my secret admirer.

Three more rounds of flooring it into the curves and the Tesla was nowhere to be seen. Was it possible? Had I actually lost this fucker?

There was a long straightaway after passing Lucia and I decided to take no chances. I pushed the roadster to one fifty and held it for as long as I could. Then I continued my practice of hitting the curves at one twenty.

Again and again, I flew around the turns and redlined down the straightaways. Talk about exhilaration—a guy could get used to this. I'd never been much of a thrill-seeker, but now I was a converted man. Nothing but roadsters for me from this day onward.

As I shot past Esalen, I prepared to pat myself on the back and declare victory. I even envisioned leading a work-shop—*Self Healing with Convertibles*—when a blur of red sidled up next to me in the oncoming traffic lane. The asshole even had the audacity to honk.

I just kept staring straight ahead and held my speed. No way was I going to look at the driver. No way was I going to acknowledge this idiot. Whatsoever.

The Tesla stuck by my side for a few seconds, then it shot ahead like some sort of flying saucer. No howling engine noise, no thunderous exhaust. Just effortless speed of the highest order. As much as I hated to admit it, a battery-powered motor had pulverized my handcrafted internal combustion engine.

I'd done enough crying for the day, so my only option was to man up. I couldn't beat the Tesla, that was for sure, but at least I could make it work for a living. I switched into 'Race' mode, set the exhaust to its loudest setting, and thrust the pedal to the floor once again.

I hadn't expected the mode change to make much of a difference. Wow, was I wrong. It was my first real encounter with g-force. My cheeks puffed out like pillows, my ribcage ached like I'd been side-whipped, and my brain froze like I'd swallowed a gallon of ice cream.

But it was all good because I was determined to save face. Obviously, my GT R couldn't do two fifty—I doubted the driver of the Tesla had the balls for that anyway—but I could do one fifty. And I did. Not through the turns, no, but every time the road straightened out, I hit my mark.

On several occasions, I even reached one sixty-five. It was on the third such time that I finally got another glimpse of red. That gave me all the motivation I needed. I could do this, I could really do this.

I executed another s-turn, entered a long straightaway, and resolved to continue onward by faith alone. I could barely see, the wind was lashing my face, and the road noise was so loud, I couldn't hear anything either. But what did I care? It was one seventy or nothing.

I dropped my foot like a lead weight, white-knuckled the steering wheel, and let my vehicle pursue its destiny. Five more minutes of faith-driving and there it was—the red Tesla, only a stone's throw in front of me.

What followed unfurled so fast that it actually felt slow. I'm not sure which one of us saw the yellow first, but the sight was certainly more impressive coming from the south. Of course, I had the advantage because I'd seen it already: DELIAH, spray-painted in big yellow letters on a boulder by the side of the road.

The Tesla seemed to be heading straight for the graffiti. But why would the driver be drawn to it? What would it mean to anyone besides me? Didn't the idiot realize there was a hundred-foot precipice directly behind it?

At first, I thought the vehicle was going to ram into the defaced mass of granite. But then it veered at the last possible instant. Instead of striking the boulder, it hit the guardrail to the left.

The flimsy guardrail was no match for two tons of hurtling machinery. The red roadster cut through it like butter. But what I hadn't noticed before was a ramp-like mound of compacted soil behind the guardrail.

The Tesla hit the ramp at one fifty and launched like a

Cobra missile. It only maintained its velocity for an instant, but my whole world inverted at the apex of its arc. Because the occupant suddenly stood up on his driver's seat and performed a perfect swan dive, ejecting into mid-air. And that was when I finally saw who the maniac was—god damn motherfucking John Laster.

There was no time to process, no time to think, no time to reason through the situation. There was only time to feel. And contrary to all prevailing logic, all human rationality, all dialectical inquiry, what I felt was the urge to follow after him.

I'd already been driving by faith, so it wasn't that much of a stretch. Like I'd told Bunni, I loved John Laster. Of all the men I'd ever known, he was the only one who'd ever truly helped me navigate the labyrinth of humanity. Why not let him navigate for me now—when I was at the most challenging crossroads of my life, when Deliah needed me the most, when Alex needed me the most, when my soul needed me the most?

In truth, it was the easiest decision I ever made. I simply steered the GT R toward the same ramp John had used and turned over my life to fate. I couldn't see a thing beyond the boulder. There was no way to tell where I would fall—on land or water, rocks or tidepools, heaven or earth—and I was okay with that.

Just like John, I hit the ramp at one fifty. Just like John, I stood on the driver's seat when the GT R reached the apex of its arc. And just like John, I performed a swan dive, ejecting into mid-air.

As I hurtled through the Big Sur sky, I said goodbye to

my beloved roadster—the one earthly thing I loved almost as much as Alex and Deliah and John and Bunni.

And then I fell and I fell and I fell some more.

TWENTY-EIGHT

Reversing It

In the span of less than a second, I lived another lifetime. All my issues with my mother and father were resolved. All my relationship problems were overcome. All my questions about the meaning of life were answered. All my fears of death were dissolved.

And when I plunked into the sea—when my second life ended and my first life reverted—I felt the hard smack of the water on my skull, but I didn't take it seriously. How could I? How could anything feel as serious as it once had?

Descending into the icy cold water, I kept my eyes open. It was the deepest blue I'd ever seen. I'd never known a blue so cold and beautiful and dark all at once.

I had no compulsion to breathe, no desire to move my limbs or propel myself in any way. Why interfere with the blue? What could be better than receiving its pureness?

After a seeming eternity, I felt a hand reach for my forearm. My first instinct was to resist, but I sensed a benevolence in the warmth of the touch and I yielded. A human began tugging me purposefully to the surface of the water.

It was John Laster. When my head finally bobbed above the water, I stared at him with big, round bug eyes and a beatific smile. He implored me to intake oxygen, but I couldn't comprehend his fervor.

"Breathe, Paul!" he screamed.

I wanted to comply if only to please my dear friend. But I no longer had any control over my lungs. And I was okay with that.

"Breathe!"

We looked to be about a hundred yards from shore. There was no beach in sight, just sheer cliffs rising from fast-moving and turbulent water. Waves crashed violently against the cliffs, sending huge sprays in our direction. The water surrounding us was relatively calm, however, as we were past the impact zone.

John wrapped his arms around me from behind and, treading water furiously, tilted me on my back. He alternated between administering chest compressions and rescue breaths. For the first three rounds, his efforts had no effect. Performing CPR in the open water seemed a hopeless task.

On the fourth round, however, I felt an odd, tickling sensation rise up from my chest. John initiated another compression and I managed to expel a mouthful of water. He breathed into my mouth again and I remembered how to use my lungs.

"Love!" I gasped, as I sucked in air.

"Yes!" screamed Laster. "That's it, Paul!"

"Love!" I shouted again, laughing and breathing at the same time.

"You're okay, Paul!"

John proceeded to demonstrate how to float on his back. I imitated him and was surprised by how well it worked. Once on my back, I barely needed to kick with my feet, thanks to the buoyancy of the saltwater.

"The current will carry us southward," he explained. "There should be a beach in a couple of miles."

"It's okay if there's not," I gurgled. "It's all okay."

As we floated, I stared up at the sky. It was a lighter blue than the ocean, but still surprisingly dark. A California condor passed overhead. Humpback whales breached and spouted in the distance.

Still on our backs, we drifted by an enormous kelp forest. John held my hand to make sure I steered clear of the kelp. He said we could get tangled in it if we got too close.

As we continued, a family of otters came within a few feet of us. The father and mother were on their backs, like John and I. The pup cavorted amongst us and seemed to consider hopping onto me until one of the parents intervened.

We rounded a bend in the coastline and glimpsed a sandy beach. I'd been calm until that moment, but when I imagined what it would feel like to be supported by land, I panicked. Frantically, I began swimming toward the shore.

John shook his head and yelled for me to stop, but I ignored him and kept swimming. He followed after me reluctantly, not wanting us to become separated. After a few dozen strokes, I fatigued, realizing the distance was further than I'd estimated.

"Just relax," said John. "The current will do the work."

We returned to floating on our backs and, after a few

minutes, I noticed I was able to touch the ground. John put his arm around me and together we walked ashore. We sat down on a warm, sunny bank of sand.

"You saved my life," I said. "Thank you."

"I'm afraid I risked it more than I saved it," he replied.

I considered asking him for clarification, but at that moment we heard the loud whir of a helicopter. John waved his hands to catch the pilot's attention. The helicopter circled around us once and touched down on the sand. An emergency medical technician jumped out and walked briskly toward us.

"Which one of you is John Laster?" he asked.

"That would be me," said Laster. "And this is my good friend, Paul Wolniak."

We shook hands and made small talk as the EMT began checking our vitals. Two other crew members emerged from the helicopter. They began taking photographs and jotting down notes.

"You both appear to be okay," said the EMT, after conducting several tests. "No signs of hypothermia or cardiac arrest."

"Glad to hear it," I replied.

"The vehicles are fully submerged, I presume?" he asked.

"Correct," said Laster.

"Impact was approximately three clicks northwest?"

"Sounds about right."

"We'll send out a diving crew. No need for you to stick around for that. Might as well get you boarded and on your way."

"Much appreciated," replied Laster. "Can you drop us in

hit me like a ton of bricks. Every single thing that had happened to me since I'd found Deliah's Post It Note had been carefully orchestrated—by *her*.

Going forward, I had to make sure I stayed exactly on the path she intended for me. Because what was now painfully obvious was that she'd thought through this chess game a million times better than I had.

I reached out to shake Laster's hand. "Thanks, John," I said. "I'll play this the way you're saying."

"I knew there was a reason I like you so much," he replied. "Elon's going to be a little bummed that I trashed his demo vehicle, but we're having some crazy fun, aren't we?"

"Hell, yeah, we are."

"So here's what I suggest. You drive on up to Palo Alto, as planned. But you treat Deliah's father like you know nothing. Don't give him the slightest tip-off. Instead, smother him with kindness. And when the opportunity presents itself, work the mom for intel instead of the dad. But make sure you're a hundred percent discreet about it, okay?"

It was good advice and I knew it. I realized I didn't just love John. I actually trusted him.

"You got it," I said. "I'm totally on board." We high-fived each other and I took a long swig of Gatorade.

As I did, the helicopter touched down at the Palo Alto airport. Two silver Porsche Cayennes were parked next to the heliport. The pilot got up from the cockpit and handed John an envelope and some keys.

"I trust these vehicles will be suitable?"

"Perfect, Captain," said John. "Perfect."

"Thanks, everyone," I called out. "Have a great day."

We disembarked and walked toward the Porsches. John

tossed me one of the keys and slipped me the envelope. I looked inside and saw a wad of cash.

"It's just a little spending money, so you can get some clothes. I had Alex pack up a suitcase for you, but I'm afraid it's at the bottom of the sea."

"I don't know what to say," I replied, flabbergasted.

"If you need anything else, don't hesitate to call. We'll reconvene in a day or two."

"I owe you, John. You've been insanely helpful."

He shrugged his shoulders. "Time will tell."

"Come to think of it," I said, "I do have a small bone to throw your way."

"Oh?"

"Alex said you own painsluts.com."

"Yeah, I dabbled in websites before the dispensaries."

"Well, I had an insight while I was underwater."

"I'm all ears."

"You know how you use an algorithm to decide the next video to stream to users after they finish watching one?"

"Sure, I paid a few million for that algorithm."

"Why don't you try reversing it?"

"Reversing it?"

"Yeah, instead of feeding them a video that best matches their stated preferences and usage patterns, feed them one that is the exact opposite. Don't take them to the light. Take them to the shadow. You follow me?"

"Fuckin' A, Paul Wolniak. It's not a bad idea."

And with that, I gave him a salute, hopped into my Cayenne, and headed off to avenge Deliah—however the hell she wanted me to do so.

TWENTY-NINE

One Wilted Plumeria

My phone didn't survive the Big Sur plunge, so I decided to show up unannounced at Walter and Iolana's house. On the way there, I shopped at a Ross Dress For Less in Seaside. I doubted it was what John had in mind—the envelope he'd given me contained fifteen thousand dollars—but I was a simple man with simple tastes.

The moment I pulled up to their home in the Porsche Cayenne, Walter came barreling out of the front door. "Please don't tell me you swapped the Mercedes for that SUV!" he cried.

"No," I replied, grinning. "It's just a loaner. The Mercedes is in the shop."

"Thank god. So we still have ourselves a deal?"

"Yes, Walter. The roadster will be yours very soon."

"Excellent. In that case, I can invite you in."

I shook his hand, trying not to show my disdain for his corrupted soul. As we walked into the house, Iolana gave me a warm hug. Not a trace remained of the blame she'd once harbored toward me.

"What brings you to our neck of the woods, Paul?" she asked.

"I had a job interview if you could call it that, so I thought I'd swing by to see how you're doing."

"What a nice surprise. I'm grilling wild sea bass and there's more than enough for you to join us."

"Uh, I'm not sure about that, Yo-Yo," protested Walter. "I played a full round of golf today and I need my protein."

"Hush, dear," she replied. "You'll get as much as you want."

We chatted about weather, politics, and healthcare as Iolana prepared the meal. Walter insisted on simultaneously listening to the nightly news, ignoring Iolana's plea to lower the volume. Her solution was to move us to the outdoor patio table.

Nothing of significance was said over dinner, but the food was tasty and the conversation civil. Green beans and fingerling potatoes supplemented the sea bass. Walter had a second helping, but I politely declined.

For dessert, we sipped port and nibbled on bread pudding. Walter told the same joke he'd recounted on my last visit—it was a decent one and I laughed just as hard as the first time. Then he settled into his La-Z-Boy recliner in the living room and promptly fell asleep.

"If now is an okay time," I said to Iolana, "I'd love to see that scrapbook you put together."

"Of course, dear," she replied. "I'm sorry you had to wait this long."

"It's okay. I don't think I was quite ready last time."

"Grief has its own timetable."

"Very true," I agreed.

We moved to the dining table, where she set the scrapbook in front of me, and I began flipping through the pages. The photos were arranged chronologically, starting with Deliah's birth. By her preschool years, a boy with red hair began appearing regularly. I said nothing about the boy, instead commenting on how cute Deliah looked.

When they entered kindergarten, the two children were assigned the same teacher. If the scrapbook was any indication, Deliah and the red-haired boy became virtually inseparable. There were photos of them swimming together, climbing trees together, riding bikes together—all the usual things best friends did.

The pattern continued until Deliah reached the third grade. Early in that year, the pictures of the boy came to an abrupt halt. The last photo in which they both figured was a sleepover at Deliah's house. They were in their pajamas, building an indoor fort out of cardboard boxes.

"Who's the red-headed kid?" I finally asked.

"Just some neighborhood boy. I forget his name."

"He shows up in almost every photo and now, poof, I'm not seeing him anymore."

Iolana shook her head. "I dunno. I guess he moved away or something."

"Are you sure?" I looked her straight in her eyes.

"Why are you so interested?" she countered.

"Truth be told?"

She shrugged.

"I think I met this person recently," I said. "We've become friends."

Iolana looked at me for a long time without showing any emotion. Then her chest heaved and her eyes began to turn red. "You know Alex?" she asked. "You've been in touch with him?"

"Yes," I said, nodding my head. "Except he's a she now."

She looked dumbfounded at first, but her confusion soon turned to concern. "How is the poor child?"

"She's doing well, considering everything. But she's been through hell. I suspect you know that."

"Oh, Paul," she murmured, choking back tears, "I can't be talking about this. I just can't. Especially not with him here." She gestured toward Walter.

"I wouldn't exactly say he's here. He's out like a light. But if it makes you feel better, how about we move outside?"

I helped her up from her chair and put my arm around her as we walked to the backyard. She led us to a gazebo where there was an outdoor couch. We sat down in the moonlight amidst the scent of jasmine flowers.

"You must hate me, Paul," she said. "You must think I'm the biggest coward ever to live."

"Not at all," I replied. "I'm sure you had very good reasons for your decisions. But what would really help now is honesty—complete honesty."

"Agreed." Her lips were trembling.

"Did you witness what happened to Alex?" I asked.

"Heavens, no, I'm not a monster. I would have stopped Walter if I'd seen it happen. I would have shot him, I think."

"But you know for sure he did it?"

"Part of me always harbored the crazy hope that maybe he didn't—that maybe none of it happened. But, in reality, I knew when I saw Alex's eyes the morning after the sleepover. I should have reported it right then and there. And certainly, when Alex didn't show up for school the next day, when he refused to return Dee's messages, I should have contacted his parents. There were so many things I should have done. I should have gone to the police, I should have divorced Walter, I should have protected my daughter. But to have done nothing, to have not dared to name the truth, to have not defended Dee's best friend, to have not admitted it was all based on a lie..."

"What was based on a lie?" I asked.

She looked at me like I'd punched her in the gut. "I can't, Paul. I can't possibly unburden myself that much."

"Yes, you can." I reached out to hold her hand. "You can and you must. Your days of keeping it all inside are gone. They're over. It's a new chapter now. Please, for Deliah and for Alex. And for me, okay?"

"You really think it's not too late? You really think it makes any difference now?"

"I do."

She wiped her eyes with a napkin and took a deep breath. "So you know how Deliah was brought into this world? You've figured out that too?"

I shook my head.

"But you can guess, right?"

The horror of what she was suggesting had never occurred to me until that moment. To even *think* the idea seemed impossible. I'd always assumed insanity could only extend so far. But when it came to human beings, the terrible, terrible truth was that there were no limits. None at all. It was a lesson I'd never been able to learn no matter how many cruelties of humankind were revealed to me.

"You understand now?" she continued.

"I think so. I need to hear you say it."

"Say it? How am I supposed to do that?"

"One word at a time. One sentence at a time."

"You make it sound so easy."

"Not easy, Iolana. Necessary."

She took another deep breath. Her eyes and face were swollen, her makeup running.

"I was only seventeen when it happened," she said tentatively. "I was born into a poor hapa family. We lived in what you'd call a shack—*hale kua*. Mom and Dad worked the sugarcane factory. Dad had a drinking problem, so they were always fighting. I never dated, never had a boyfriend, because there was no time for silly trifles like that.

"One day, I was out late in the taro fields—it was the only job a kid could get. All the other workers had quit, but I wanted to make a bit more money to please Dad. That's when a jeep rolled up next to me. Four military guys were in it. Walter was one of them. It all happened so fast, there was nothing I could do. They jumped out of the jeep, pinned me down, pushed my nose in the dirt, and Walter had his way with me."

"Oh, Iolana. I'm so sorry." I clasped her hand tightly.

"I never told anyone. Not a soul. Who could I tell? I just kept going to school and work like nothing had happened. Of course, I made sure to never be alone in the fields again. But it didn't matter. The jeep found me two more times when I was walking on the side of the road—I had no car, no friends to drive me, no other options. I tried to run when I saw the jeep, but they were big, tough men. Who was I kidding? They had me down on the ground again, nose to the dirt, in five seconds. And Walter had his way with me two more times."

"That's awful. Absolutely horrific."

"Three months passed. I had morning sickness and I was almost starting to show, but at least I hadn't seen the jeep. Just when I thought maybe it was over, a black Lincoln Town Car pulled up in front of our shack. It was Walter with his commanding officer. I heard the officer tell him, 'You do right by this woman or you'll be court-martialed. You hear me?' Walter got out of the car and the officer drove off.

"As he walked up to our house, I saw him grab a plumeria flower lying on the ground. Just any old one. It didn't matter. He knocked on the front door, got down on his knee, and handed my mom the flower. That's all it took—one wilted plumeria. We were married the next day. He never said a word to me about what he'd done. No apology, no concession, no explanation whatsoever. The only gift he gave me is that we didn't have sex even once as a married couple.

"I'll never know if it was the first, second, or third time he raped me that made Deliah. But I guess it makes no difference. She didn't come from a real marriage anyway. She came from a betrayal, a violation, a lie. That was our whole foundation. You understand now? Is that enough detail, Paul?"

I looked at Iolana in stunned silence. The moon shone above us as if it were the same moon that had been shining before she spoke. But of course, it wasn't. Nothing was the same now.

I'd asked for complete honesty and she'd provided it. But I hadn't been the slightest bit prepared. Iolana's words had upended me. They explained everything about Deliah, everything about our marriage, everything about our struggles, everything about life.

There wasn't a single action I could take in a hundred zillion years that would have been even remotely adequate as a response. We both knew that, although I'm sure Iolana knew better than I. And that was why, as trivial as it may sound, the one small thing that occurred to me to do was to pick a fresh jasmine flower and carefully place it behind her left ear.

It wasn't the last thing I did and it wasn't the only thing I did. But it was all I could do on that night, under that moon, in that aching world of sorrow, loss, and treachery.

And we both knew that too.

THIRTY

Thwack

AS A FRESHMAN IN COLLEGE, I had a biology professor who claimed human beings were the only animals who never reached maturation. I thought the distinction implied our superiority because it meant we were lifelong learners. But that morning, as I emerged from a fitful sleep in Walter and Iolana's guest room, I realized he was suggesting something else.

What my professor meant was that humans were reality distorters—and they got better at it as they aged. They became increasingly comfortable melding dark and light. The ones who were best at it, the ones who mastered rationalizing their behavior, often became rich and powerful while wreaking havoc on those around them.

Walter was one of those supreme distorters. He believed his victims weren't sentient beings. He believed his victims wanted to be raped. He believed they needed to be raped.

In my view, rape almost surpassed murder as a crime because it left the victim's mind and body intact to continue reliving the violation over and over again. I wanted Walter to pay in a way that fully recognized the lifelong damage rape caused. But it wasn't my call to make.

I had to keep reminding myself of what John had advised. I was at Walter and Iolana's house on an intel-gathering mission, nothing else. I'd already accomplished a great deal, but there was more work to be done.

With that in mind, I put on my most pleasant smiley face and headed down to breakfast. Iolana was cooking bacon and eggs while Walter read the morning paper. Everything seemed perfectly normal—as if there'd been no earth shattering revelations the prior night.

"Good morning, son," said Walter.

"Good morning," I replied.

"How'd you sleep?" asked Iolana.

"Just fine. And you two?"

"Oh, we don't need much sleep anymore," she answered. "One of the benefits of aging."

"Speak for yourself," said Walter. "I got my beauty rest and I'm ready to hit the golf course. Care to join me, Paul?"

Iolana gestured that I didn't need to go, but I saw it as an opportunity. "I'd love to," I replied, "as long as you don't mind playing with a bogey golfer."

"Are you kidding? A man in your prime and you're only a mid-handicapper? Well, I guess I'll just have to enjoy whooping your ass."

I laughed demurely and, as soon as we finished breakfast, Walter whisked me away to the Palo Alto Hills Golf & Country Club. The setting was stunningly beautiful. I'd only played public golf courses in Los Angeles, which were in a whole other league, and I quickly got swept into the game.

Fortunately, Walter was in a chatty mood. Without my even trying to direct the conversation, he ending up spilling all kinds of information. At first, it was mostly about his career accomplishments, but on the 14th hole, he started talking about Deliah.

"You were lucky to have been married to her, son," he said, as he sunk a putt. "You know that, right?"

"Absolutely, she was an amazing wife. More than I ever could have hoped for."

"I have a little confession to make," he continued. "I always was a bit jealous of you."

"Jealous? Why?" My putt sped past the hole.

"You know, son. She was quite an attractive woman, wouldn't you agree?"

"Oh, yes, she certainly was."

"And since it's just us boys out here, you don't mind me speaking freely, do you?"

"Of course not," I said.

My stomach started doing backflips, but I knew I had to play it cool or I'd blow the whole thing. I feigned a grin and watched Walter take a chip shot. To his credit, he landed the ball in the hole.

"Yee doggy!" he exclaimed. "It's a sign!"

"What happens on the golf course, stays on the golf course, right?"

"I like you, son. I really like you."

"I'm just sorry we didn't get to spend more time like this while Deliah was alive," I added for effect.

"Me too, but you know there was a reason why I kept my distance those years. Did Dee ever talk to you about that?"

"No, never."

"Yeah, I wouldn't have expected her to, but we didn't exactly have the typical father-daughter relationship."

"Oh?" I pulled out a 5-wood and made a mediocre distance shot, missing the hole by about fifty yards.

"It was a bit more personal than that," he explained. "I guess I'm sort of feeling you out here. Do you follow me, son?"

"I think I do, Walter. And honestly, you don't need to fear any judgment from me. I understand how complicated the world can get. Nothing is cookie-cutter simple like they try to sell us on TV."

"I'm glad you said that."

"No worries." I was pleased with myself at how well I was rolling with the madness, so I just kept going. "We all have our secrets."

"That's exactly what I was driving at," replied Walter, "so it must be time to pull out my driver." We both laughed and he took his swing, knocking the ball a good two hundred and eighty yards.

"Nice one," I said.

"You know, son, I sometimes took Dee on road trips when she was a teenager. Just me and her. We left Yo-Yo behind."

"Oh, yeah?"

"Sometimes the motel rooms only had one bed. It wasn't anything I planned, see, it just happened. But like I said, Deliah was an attractive woman. And Yo-Yo and I didn't exactly have an intimate marriage, as you might have guessed."

"That can happen." I made another bad putt, and another, until I finally got the ball in the hole.

"So you understand then, right?" he said. "There are desires a man has that can't always be denied. Even when the lady isn't quite so enthusiastic."

"I get what you're saying, I do."

"And there's my heritage too. Did Dee ever tell you that my family roots trace back to the Swedish slave trade?"

"She never mentioned that, no."

"One side captained the slave ships, the other made the iron chains."

"Wow, that's quite a legacy."

"Sometimes having a background like that gives a man ideas. You know what I mean?"

"Uh-huh, sure."

We were on the 18th hole and it was my turn to drive. I probably should have kept working Walter, but I felt like I was about to puke. I had no subterfuge left in me whatsoever. None.

I teed the ball and checked my stance, desperately trying not to think about what Walter had confessed. Just play golf, I told myself. I hovered the clubhead above the ground, exhaled all the breath from my lungs, and took my best swing. Thwack.

The ball lifted high into the sky. It couldn't have been more lined up—not because I was a good golfer, no, but because I was a crazed golfer. A crazed and outraged and eviscerated golfer who had just discovered why his ex-wife had never been able to love him.

We both watched in awe as the ball climbed to its apex and floated like a delicate songbird to its intended target. It was a hole in one. Picture perfect.

Evidently, there was a god lingering around somewhere in this mad world because at that point our discourse came to an immediate halt. Walter stormed off the fairway, sulking like a baby, and we exchanged no further words for the remainder of our outing.

I'd never been so glad to stop talking in all my life.

THIRTY-ONE

Umbilically Connected

ON THE DRIVE back to Walter and Iolana's place, I remained polite, not giving the slightest clue that I was horrified beyond belief. Walter got over his tantrum in short order and he began delivering a steady stream of one-liners to which I laughed appropriately. It was business as usual.

When we got home, I continued to maintain my façade of cheerfulness. We shared the highlights of our golf game with Iolana and I affirmed all of Walter's achievements. Neither one of us mentioned my hole-in-one shot.

Iolana could tell something alarming had happened, but she was just as skillful as me at hiding her awareness. We waited patiently until after dinner when, once again, Walter collapsed on his La-Z-Boy recliner. Then we returned to the outdoor couch under the gazebo.

"What'd he say to you?" she asked nervously.

"He didn't bring up anything about you or Alex," I replied. "Instead, he talked about his relationship with Deliah."

"With Deliah?" She mopped her forehead with her hand.

"He implied that he had sex with her on multiple occasions. I assume you knew that, right?"

"What? That's insane, he couldn't possibly have. I watched him like a hawk her whole childhood."

I studied her face to measure her certainty. "The road trips he took with her when she was a teenager," I said. "Do those ring a bell?"

"Road trips? I never would've allowed that. I'm not an idiot."

"He said they went to motels where there was just one bed. He pretty much gave a full rape confession, even admitting that he forced her against her wishes."

Iolana let out a whimper of agony. "But I was always home. How could he have taken her to motels without me knowing?"

"You never went away anywhere by yourself? Never went to visit your parents or anything like that?"

Suddenly, she looked at me in shock. "Oh, god in heaven," she groaned. "When I was diagnosed with breast cancer, I had to be hospitalized overnight a few times. The mastectomy didn't go as expected. There were complications. Dee was a teenager when it happened."

"He's a monster," I said. "A fucking monster."

She burst into tears. "I never thought he'd be capable of doing something like that when I was in such a vulnerable state, when I was suffering so much. If I had, I wouldn't have checked into the hospital. I would have just stayed home and let the cancer take me. I swear it, Paul. You've got to believe me."

"I believe you, Iolana. It's okay. It's not your fault. He's a predator, a psychopathic predator."

"All these years, I never was able to face facts about what I was dealing with," she sobbed. "And now look at the damage I caused. I'm such a horrible person."

"No, you're not a horrible person. You're a wonderful person and a wonderful mother. But Walter's an expert at what he does. He knows exactly how to manipulate outcomes to get what he wants."

"That's true. He does. And I've played right into his hand this whole time." She continued her sobbing.

"Which is why I need you to take a deep breath and focus. So once and for all, we can turn this around."

She inhaled deeply, wiping away her tears. "Okay, Paul. I'll try to hold it together. I will."

"Before going further, I need to ask you an important question. Do you want to do something about this situation? Or do you just want to survive it?"

"What on earth could I possibly do? I've never been able to think of anything all these years."

"I'm not asking for you to figure out what to do, I'm asking if you *want* to do something."

"Of course, I want to do something. I've wanted to do something ever since the first time I had my nose shoved in the dirt. But what's a housewife like me supposed to do? What options do I have?"

"I'm in the process of figuring that out. I need to do some poking around. Are you okay with that?"

"Yes," she sniffled. "Whatever you think would help."

"Good." I paused to take a deep breath of my own. "This might seem like a strange question, but has Walter ever mentioned his family's history in the Swedish slave trade?"

"Ughh, yes, too much. It's almost like he's proud of it or something. I made him throw away all his family heirlooms that go back to those days, except he still keeps a disgusting piece of iron chain on his desk. He says it's from the 1700s, made at his family's factory. He's always holding it, moving it from one hand to the other. It turns my stomach every time. It was used to shackle slaves, but he refuses to get rid of it no matter how much I plead with him."

"Does he have other family members he discusses this stuff with?"

"I don't think so, at least not that I know of. He fiddles online from time to time, but I don't pay much attention. I'm just glad when he's out of my hair."

"I understand. This is very, very helpful. Just one more question. Are you able to log into his laptop?"

"I'm not sure, it's been a while since I tried. Let's go see."

I followed Iolana into Walter's den. She pointed to a piece of old rusted iron chain sitting on his mahogany desk and made a mock-vomiting gesture, then she opened up his MacBook Pro. When she rested her finger on the Touch ID sensor, she was immediately granted access.

"Excellent," I said.

"He had me add my fingerprint a couple of years ago so I could check stuff for him when he was out playing golf," she explained.

"Do you know his Apple ID password too?"

"I believe so, yes."

"And will Walter be on that recliner for a while?"

"Yeah, he'll practically be in a coma until I wake him."

"So you're up for pulling an all-nighter with me?"

"I told you I don't need much sleep."

"Then let's rock and roll, Yo-Yo."

I held out my hand and we high-fived each other. She giggled nervously and I snapped my fingers, which she reciprocated. Her snap was even louder and crisper than mine, which I hadn't expected, and this time we both laughed cathartically.

In that moment, it occurred to me that she felt like a mother. An actual mother. A real mother. A mother that I'd never had.

It occurred to me that she felt like a mother to whom I would be umbilically connected all the rest of my remaining days—for better or for worse.

THIRTY-TWO

Five Hundred and Thirty-Four

For three solid hours, Iolana and I combed through Walter's laptop. We checked his emails, texts, documents, images, bookmarks, social media, and everything else we could think of that might provide clues about his nefarious activities. We also reviewed his web browser history and did a global search for terms like rape, slave, and sex.

Unfortunately, none of our efforts pointed to anything useful. Since Walter had given Iolana fingerprint access to his laptop, the outcome wasn't too surprising. I began to wonder if one of his other devices might yield more dirt. Smartphones were generally favored for encrypted communication, after all.

"Do you know where he keeps his iPhone?" I asked Iolana in a hushed voice.

"In his pants," she replied. "At all times."

"That's a problem." I rolled my eyes.

"It's okay, I can get it."

Without delay, she proceeded to extract his iPhone from the hip pocket of his chinos. All the while, he remained asleep on the recliner in blissful ignorance. She brought the phone to me with a spark of hope in her eyes that I hadn't seen before.

We ran into a minor problem logging in because it used Face ID—until we realized the obvious. Iolana positioned the phone in front of Walter's face and, by sheer luck, his eyelids were open just enough to satisfy the facial recognition software.

Once we were in, we went straight to the messaging apps. He'd installed Threema, Kik, WhatsApp, Skype, TikTok, Wire, Telegram, Signal, and WeChat—a shit ton of platforms for a man in his late sixties.

Each one had its unique difficulties when it came to accessing the secure areas. Walter's Apple password came in handy, but it wasn't good enough for the apps that used pin codes. We remained stumped for about a half-hour until we tried his birthdate. In retrospect, it was an obvious choice, given his narcissistic tendencies.

From there we hunkered down and scoured each of the areas for signs of foul play. Predictably, the first seven apps were duds, as Walter had barely used any of them. But when we came to the eighth one, Signal, we hit pay dirt.

"Holy crap," I whispered, "forty-three separate users are linked to his account and they all show recent activity."

"What's that mean?" asked Iolana.

"That we've found what we were looking for."

Signal had a reputation for being one of the most secure messaging apps on the market, as well as a strict policy of not maintaining the keys to decrypt messages, so we probably should have checked it first. We were just trying to be methodical. The problem was that it was almost three o'clock in the morning and Walter was starting to stir.

"We might only have about thirty more minutes," cautioned Iolana. "He sometimes wakes up early."

I quickly drilled down to study the content posted to the account. Each thread began with a street address. After that, there was a sequence of dates with corresponding star ratings. In some cases, an address had just one date associated with it, but in others it had as many as fourteen or fifteen. Every once in a while, an address would get updated too.

That was pretty much it. None of the threads contained any additional information. Since Signal allowed self-destructing messages, the more incriminating data had probably been purged—if it ever existed. We were lucky anything remained at all.

Using my phone, I recorded all of the linked usernames. Then I took a photograph of every thread, even though my hands were shaking like leaves. I kept telling myself not to overthink it, not to try to figure out what I was looking at, just to document everything. But in my gut, I already felt sure I knew.

Given the situation, it seemed an obvious interpretation that the addresses were locations of rape victims and the dates were the times when the victims got raped. A victim was selected by whoever posted the address. The rapes were committed by whoever posted a date.

Walter's account had posted thirteen dates in the past

eighteen months. Each account averaged about twelve dates, so he was just slightly more active than most. Altogether, there were five hundred and thirty-four dates posted by the accounts in the eighteen-month period.

In other words, what we were looking at was a circle of forty-three rapists who were using Signal not only to broadcast their rapes, but also to share their victims' locations with the rest of the circle. The purpose of the group seemed to be to encourage follow-up rapes by other members of the circle —as unfathomable as that sounded.

"Do we have everything we need?" asked Iolana nervously.

"Yes," I replied, "everything and more. Much, much more." I handed her the phone.

"Okay, I'd better put this back and help him to bed, so he doesn't get suspicious."

I nodded my head and retreated to the kitchen as she set out to perform the task. Even after everything she'd endured and all of Walter's abuses, Iolana handled the duty with supreme grace. Slowly and carefully, she helped him up to his feet and guided him to their master bedroom while he grunted and groaned in a befuddled state.

If it had been me, I probably would have shown less kindness. I probably would have dragged him down the hallway a bit more vigorously. And I probably would have let him fall into bed a bit harder. On his face, preferably.

The truth was, at that particular moment in time, I was more fucked up than I'd ever been in my whole life. In fact, it was truly laughable how little I'd been fucked up all the times I'd ever thought I was fucked up compared to how fucked up I was at that moment. That's how fucked up I was.

After all, we were talking about five hundred and thirty-four rapes. Not one. Not two. Not three. Not four. *Five hundred and thirty-four.*

And counting.

THIRTY-THREE

The Stuff with the Dildos

Filled with sadness, melancholy, and sorrow, I made my way back to Point Dume in the Porsche Cayenne. Even though I'd achieved my objective, I felt like a shell of a man, like an automaton going through the motions. I had all the answers I'd so desperately sought to explain my failed marriage, but they provided zero comfort. Zero.

Now I knew why Deliah always had that sad look on her face. Now I knew why she told me she could never really love anyone. Now I knew why she wanted a condo where she couldn't see any roads from the windows. And perhaps most importantly, now I knew why we both picked each other. Our holes from childhood offered perfect hiding grounds for each other—until they didn't.

The realizations were enough to make me want to run the Cayenne into a telephone pole and be done with it all. I'd never before seen the gruesome underbelly of humanity so clearly. But giving up now would only expand the victory for Walter and his sick group—and all the other disgusting rapists out there.

I had an obligation to Deliah, as well as to Iolana and Alex and the other victims, and I intended to see the matter to its conclusion. Whatever she wanted me to do, that's what I would do, for as long as I could continue to put one foot in front of the other. I kept telling myself that, like a mantra, for the whole drive to Point Dume.

WHEN I FINALLY PULLED INTO John's driveway and returned to what I was beginning to understand was my home, Alex raced out to greet me. She threw her arms around me, showered me with kisses, and tousled my hair. And while I couldn't shake my depressed state entirely, I felt an enormous sense of relief in her presence.

John and Bunni were almost as glad to see me. They welcomed me like a long-lost friend, each taking one of my hands and leading me through the English garden. Alex trailed behind singing "The Happy Wanderer" in the most magically soothing voice imaginable.

A veritable cornucopia of earthly delights awaited us on a hillside deck overlooking the ocean. As we dined, the three of them gave me every courtesy, every consideration of my fragile state. And slowly, gradually, I relayed my primary discoveries.

By the time I'd laid out the full scenario, they were each thoroughly appalled. None of them had been prepared for the magnitude of my report. Several times, we all stopped eating, requiring a moment of silence to absorb the gravity of the situation.

I tried to convey my findings as objectively as possible, but it was hard to push back the voice in my head that kept telling me it was hopeless, that there was no way anyone could ever combat an operation of the size and scope I'd stumbled upon. And even if it were possible, there was no undoing all the pain and suffering of the victims.

The others sensed my compromised state and they did their utmost to buoy my spirits. They plied me with praise and reassured me they would stand by me however I wished to proceed. But they also recognized the toll recent events had taken on me.

"You've been through absolute hell," said Alex. "It's completely normal to feel overwhelmed and exhausted."

"Thank you," I replied, resting my hand on her knee.

"None of us can truly know what it's like to be in your shoes," added Bunni. "But just keep in mind, we're all here for you, ready to do whatever it takes. And this man has some amazing resources at his disposal." She glanced towards John.

"Resources?" I said.

"Let me put it to you this way," replied John. "I promise that within a week, I'll know the identities of all forty-three of those accounts on Signal. Probably a lot sooner than that."

"Come on, that's not possible," I objected. "They're completely encrypted and no one's going to release the data for you. Even the people at Signal can't get that information —even if we got law enforcement involved."

"I have other methods," he said. "Faster and easier methods. So you can take a much-needed break."

"Exactly," agreed Alex. "You've done enough already."

"What methods?" I asked.

"There are a few possibilities that come to mind. It depends on whether you'd like to involve law enforcement."

"If you want my honest opinion," I replied, "legal channels seem way too slow for me and they might not produce the desired outcome anyway. But I'm still confused. You actually think that there is something we can do, realistically?"

"I don't think it," said John, "I know it."

"How can you be so sure? I don't get it."

"Would you agree that when there's a certain amount of money on the table, options start to look a little different?"

"I suppose if it's a big enough amount."

"Good, then you do understand. This won't be a cheap operation and I'm fine with that. I'm prepared to spend whatever it takes."

"That's another thing I don't entirely get. Why do you care so much?"

"Why? We're here because Deliah selected us for this job. Because of our pasts. You haven't figured that out by now?"

"He's right," said Bunni. "We all care passionately about breaking up this ring."

"But... but that's not what it seemed like to me when I first came here."

"You mean when we were fucking each other like wild banshees?" said Bunni.

"Yeah, I guess so," I replied sheepishly.

"How else were we supposed to get you to the next level?" said John. "No offense, my dear friend, but you needed a lot of direction, wouldn't you agree?"

I paused to digest his comment. "Are you telling me that the stuff with the dildos was all staged?"

"Hell, no!" said Bunni. "Not for a second."

"Hell, yes!" said John. "Every bit of it."

They both beamed me huge smiles and Alex erupted into laughter. Then Bunni started laughing and John started laughing. And I kind of, sort of, began to get the picture—the whole, big picture.

Because I started laughing too. Laughing, laughing, laughing. At the mystery, at the possibility, at the beauty, at the hope. And even at the sorrow.

THIRTY-FOUR

One and One and One

Even though I'd only been separated from Alex for two days, it felt like months. I was exhausted beyond belief and I didn't have a drop of energy left to think about the task ahead. All I wanted was her smooth skin pressed up against me.

"Where do you want to sleep tonight?" I asked her, as soon as we parted ways with John and Bunni.

"Anywhere is fine," she replied, kissing me on the forehead, "as long as you're there."

"Good answer," I said, "because we have some serious catching up to do."

"Yes, and Mr. Super Sleuth Detective has earned a special surprise too." She fondled my crotch and gave me a mischievous look that instantly rekindled my energy.

"I like the sound of that."

"Seriously, John wanted me to tell you he has something waiting for you in the bungalow."

"What is it?"

"I don't know, silly. It wouldn't be a surprise if he told me. But he sure seemed excited, judging from the way his eyes were sparkling."

"Damn, so I guess that means we have to walk all the way there before I can throw you down on the bed and fuck you."

"Who says we have to walk?" She giggled and started sprinting.

I raced after her, but this time I let her set the pace. It felt oddly significant to have run from the bungalow just two days ago and now to be running back to it. Nothing substantive had changed in the outer world, but everything had changed in my inner world.

When I stuck the key in the hole and pushed open the door to the bungalow, I immediately saw a Post It Note on the dining room table. It wasn't lilac colored—just the standard yellow—but still my default response was fear.

"That's the surprise?" I said.

Alex squeezed my hand. "I don't know. Let's see."

She read it aloud to me:

It's up there. Your key will work. But first these.

Drawn above the words was an upward-pointing arrow. Next to the note were two rainbow-colored gummies. That was it. Nothing else.

"What the hell," I said. "I don't get it."

"He wants us to eat the gummies and then go up somewhere."

"Yeah, but up where? We don't exactly have wings."

"Maybe we're supposed to check out the bluffs above the

bungalow. There might be a lockbox or something that your key will open."

The old me would have had doubts. The old me would have felt sabotaged that John's note stood in the way of taking Alex to bed. But the new me had no interest in indulging my doubts and fears. I simply popped one of the gummies in my mouth and offered the other one to Alex.

"Someone's feeling spontaneous today," she said approvingly.

She tossed hers into her mouth and, with a seductive grin, began sucking and chewing it. I did likewise while we stared into each other's eyes. When the tension became unbearable, I threw my arms around her and pushed my groin against her.

"Can I taste yours?" I whispered in her ear.

"Of course," she replied. "Mine is an equal-opportunity gummy."

I swirled my tongue inside her mouth. She tilted her head back, allowing me to explore more deeply. I'd never been so turned on from French kissing.

"Your gummy is better than mine," I said, after finally coming up for air.

"Maybe, but nothing tastes better than you."

I laughed and ran my hand through her hair. "We'd better go hunting for this treasure chest before I get too distracted."

"First one to find it wins," she said.

She charged out of the bungalow and onto a winding path that led up the bluffs. I followed after her, marveling at the beauty of the terrain. As we climbed higher, we enjoyed whitewater views of Paradise Cove.

At the top of the bluffs, the path leveled off and the landscaping became lusher. There was a locked gate that marked the entrance to the estate associated with the bungalow. A mosaic archway over the gate proclaimed, "Il Castello dell'Anima."

"I guess we shouldn't go past here, right?" I asked.

"I don't know. Does your key work?"

Although I was concerned we might be trespassing, I couldn't help fishing out my key and testing it. To my surprise, it turned the deadbolt. I pushed open the gate and was treated to a glimpse of a mind-bogglingly gorgeous Tuscan villa.

"Oh, man," I said. "This hurts. This really hurts my eyes."

"It's unbelievable," agreed Alex.

"I've literally had dreams about a place like this. Many, many dreams."

Alex ran past me and headed for the villa. "Come on, keep your eyes open for lockboxes."

I followed after her, mesmerized by the verdant beauty everywhere I looked. I didn't see any lockboxes, but alongside the pathway was a babbling brook bordered by wildflowers of every color. Several deer with their fawns were feeding in a pastoral meadow.

The villa itself was classic perfection with travertine walls, terracotta roof tiles, rustic wood beams, and turquoise shutters. An Olympic-sized infinity pool occupied the rear courtyard, along with a meticulously tended rose garden. Artful sculptures of majestic animals adorned the walkways.

"Is this real?" I asked. "Or are the gummies already working?"

Alex stopped to sniff a rose. "It's definitely real!"

Unable to contain myself, I ran around the perimeter of the villa. The structure was enormous, over ten thousand square feet by my estimation, but everything was in tasteful proportion. At the entrance stood two ornately carved wooden doors.

"This is crazy," I told Alex, who was close at my heels, "but I can't stop myself."

Shuddering in excitement, I inserted my key into the front door lock. Alex flashed me a smile and crossed both her fingers. I turned the key and—insanity of insanities—it met no resistance.

"What?" cried Alex. "It actually works?"

"Go ahead," I said. "You do the honors."

She pushed open the door to reveal a striking interior drenched in sunlight and impeccably decorated—not too lavishly but not too sparsely either—with an eclectic mix of Spanish, Italian, French, and Moroccan furniture.

"Hello?" I called out.

Alex didn't bother waiting for a reply. She bounded inside and began scoping out the house. I followed after her cautiously, worried there might be somebody home.

"Guess what?" shouted Alex. "There's another Post It Note on the dining room table." She proceeded to read it to me:

Welcome. And congratulations. The house is all yours. It's just a small advance for the work you did on the algorithm. We'll discuss a more proper compensation package tomorrow. —John

Next to the note were two key fobs and a deed of trust showing me as the sole owner of the villa. The property was described as a 3.54-acre parcel consisting of a 12,345 square foot home with eleven bedrooms and twelve bathrooms, as well as the bungalow, the pool, a tennis court, and a recording studio.

"Now I know it's the gummies," I said. "I'm hallucinating like crazy."

"Me too. We might as well have fun with it, right?"

Alex took my hand and led me through the kitchen to the garage. She opened the door to reveal a vast space, easily big enough to accommodate ten cars. My Travato occupied the largest bay. A brand new Solarbeam Yellow AMG GT R was parked next to it.

Scrawled on a Post It Note affixed to the hood was another message:

I trust this is a satisfactory replacement.

"It's official," I announced, as I ran my fingers along the gleaming roadster. "I have absolutely no understanding of reality."

"Nor do I, Master. Nor do I."

The edges of the Solarbeam Yellow began melting into the floor of the garage. I took Alex in my arms and my perceptual concerns vanished. We kissed and kissed and kissed.

"I need to fuck you," I said. "Right now."

"I need you to fuck me too, Master. But only if you promise me one thing—please take me in each and every one of the eleven bedrooms."

"That's a no-brainer, my sweet slutgirl. Plus I'm going to give you a bonus. I'm going to fuck you in all eleven bedrooms and the kitchen and the dining room and the living room—and even this garage too."

Clearly, the gummy was taking effect. After all my melancholy, it felt good to express such confidence.

"Oh, Master. That sounds like a dream come true."

I gently tilted Alex onto her back, so that she was sprawled on the hood of the new roadster. Then I lifted her legs over her head, raised her dress, and slid off her panties. With one quick plunge, I entered her silken pussy. Instantly, my entire world became pure, unadulterated bliss. Yet even so, with the discipline of a Zen master, I retracted my pleasure wand.

"That's it for the garage," I said.

"Oh, Master, please just a little bit more."

I ignored her request, instead scooping her into my arms and carrying her to the kitchen, where I deposited her on the breakfast nook. I gave her pussy two hard, fast strokes and immediately returned to nirvana.

"Is that better, my sexy sub?"

"Only if you don't stop, Master. Please don't stop."

"Oh, but I must. There are so many more rooms to explore."

I withdrew again and led her by the arm to a sumptuous, faux-fur couch in the living room. Playfully, I took a seat and let her ride my erection cowgirl-style. She achieved five or six joyous undulations before I lifted her off of me.

"Master, Master, you're driving me mad."

"I'm a man of my word, dearest one. The dining room beckons."

Dripping with lust, we sidled to a cavernous room with a long wooden table that seated twenty-four. Alex bent over, resting her hands on the table, and I took her from behind. The angle felt so good that I gave her ten hard strokes. I ached for more, as did she, but in spite of the purple-teal clouds upon which we now seemed to float, I knew pacing was the name of the game.

We continued in this fashion as we worked our way through each of the bedrooms of the villa. Sometimes I fucked her in the pussy, sometimes the mouth, sometimes the ass, and sometimes all three. No matter which portal of lust I chose, she was transformatively magnificent, yet I continued to resist the temptation to indulge beyond ten strokes.

So fantastical was our coupling, I couldn't begin to parse the experience. How much of it was caused by the gummies, how much by the excitement of suddenly owning a fifty million dollar seaside villa, how much by our hedonistic sampling of every room, and how much by the emotional roller coaster of the past few days?

All I knew was that I felt closer to Alex than ever. The madness of the human condition no longer dominated my awareness. Warm, slippery, succulent, psychedelic love—abundant and ubiquitous—was what filled my consciousness.

"I wonder what's in those gummies?" I asked Alex, as we initiated bedroom number five. "It feels different than the cannabis blend we had."

"Everlasting cumstopper!" she exclaimed. "You can fuck me forever and never have to cum!"

"Really? In the gummies?"

"Go ask Alice if you don't believe me."

"Alice?"

"Of course!" She cackled wildly. "Didn't you know we're in *Alice in Wonderland?*"

Or was it *Willy Wonka and the Chocolate Factory*, I wondered? Everything felt animated and fuzzy and sublime. And I seemed to possess super-human control of my erection. I no longer had any need to stop after ten strokes. I could tell exactly how close I was to orgasming and adjust accordingly.

"I see what you mean!" I cried out. "You feel soooooooo good!"

I continued fucking her with abandon. She wailed in ecstasy, almost operatically. Together, we kept climbing higher and higher. I'd never before felt even half as much joy.

"Oh, god, oh, god, oh god," squealed Alex. "I'm cumming, Master. I'm cumming soooooooooooooo hard!"

"What about the everlasting cumstopper?"

"Oh, Master, I can't stop! I'm still cumming! I'm cumming harder than I ever have! It feels so good!"

Excited beyond all measure, I rammed my cock into her again. I was dangerously close to orgasm myself, but somehow I managed to resist it as if I now had mastery of my body at the cellular level. Whoomp—I gave Alex another thrust, my hardest one of all.

"Master, Master, Master! Ooooooooooh! I'm going to squirt all over you!"

And she did. She bathed me with her Amrita fluid, her nectar of pure light and abundant love. It was indisputable— I was in the presence of a divine being, a true goddess.

In any normal world, I would have lost it at such a sight. But when Alex recovered from her empyrean release, I only wanted to give her more pleasure. I stroked her hair, her forehead, her temples, I drenched her in kisses, and I carried her to bedroom six, seven, eight, and nine, where I took her relentlessly and audaciously in slow and succulent succession.

When it came to anal sex, however, I found myself holding back. As much as I hated to admit it, my residual trauma still held sway over me. I pounded her heartily, I enjoyed her slippery smooth tightness, but I couldn't seem to put my all into the act.

Then we entered bedroom number ten and I heard a voice as clear as day commanding me to rise to the occasion. "She's giving you the greatest gift on earth, Paul. Take the gift or step aside and let another have it!"

It was the first time I'd ever looked at the world that way. Our brief stay on this crazy earth wasn't about the events that happened to us. It was about what we *did* in response to them. And if the response was sub-par, if the response was not sufficiently original, who was to blame?

Alex must have intuited what was occurring in my being because we both started crying. But the strangest thing was that there was nothing we needed to say, there was nothing we needed to do. Physically, I didn't alter the way I was fucking her ass. All I did was change the way I was feeling about it.

With one synaptic firing, I let go of all the shame, fear, doubt, and insecurity that was gripping me. I simply replaced it with gratitude—immense gratitude for the opportunity to be sharing the moment with Alex. Immense gratitude that we both were willing to be so vulnerable with each other.

Our tears drying, I continued pumping her slowly and deliberately and consistently. We floated together in a cocoon of bliss for who knows how long. And then, ever so delicately, Alex came again and she sprayed me again too.

We both were so complete, we no longer felt any need to further explore the villa. We could have stopped right there and all would have been fine. But even so, we somehow found ourselves in the eleventh bedroom.

It happened to be the biggest bedroom of all, the Master bedroom, with the best light and the best ocean views. The room literally vibrated love. No doubt, it had perfect feng shui.

Someone had removed the Kali sculpture from the Travato and placed it on the fireplace mantel as a welcoming gesture. I was still hard, still filled with lust, and I went to recline on the bed. But Alex was drawn to inspect the Kali.

She lifted it off the mantel and studied it from all sides. Then she did something I'd never done. She turned the Kali upside down and peered at the bottom.

There was a circular cork plug, which she removed to expose a large opening at the base. From within this chamber, she extracted what appeared to be a gun. It was fashioned out of smooth, pink-colored glass and the barrel was shaped like a phallus.

"What have we here?" asked Alex.

"That's super weird."

"It's sort of sexy, don't you think?" She twirled it in her hands and began to approach me. "It's giving me ideas."

"What kind of ideas?"

"There's a part of your body I haven't explored yet."

"Huh?"

"Don't worry. I'll be very gentle."

She crawled between my legs, but instead of taking my cock into her mouth, as she had done so many times before, she began to tease my perineum with her fingers. My instinct was to turn away and resist her advances, but the voice would have none of that. "Don't you remember what I told you about receiving a gift?" it boomed.

"Uh-huh," I said timidly.

While her fingers traced delicate circles around the rim of my ass, she dripped saliva between my cheeks. I braced myself as if a nurse was giving me a tetanus shot and the voice screeched, "It's a gift, Paul, not a punishment. Let the light enter."

I couldn't deny it. What Alex was doing actually felt good. She wasn't an intruder, she wasn't a rapist, she was a goddess. A divine goddess of love. All I needed to do was surrender.

She began to insert the tip of her finger in my anus. As I relaxed, she slid the finger deeper, then pulled it out, circled the rim, and reinserted it. She was using the same strategy on me that I'd used on her. I almost laughed, but I was too entranced.

Little by little, she extended her exploration until she had two fingers, three fingers, even four fingers inside me. And I didn't resist her at all. The sensation was unlike anything I'd ever felt before, and my cock was beyond hard, beyond engorged. It felt like it was made of marble.

"This ass is hungry for love," cooed Alex, "so hungry for love. Do you feel that, Master?"

I understood what she meant and I nodded my head, but I was way too high—both from the gummy and from her touch—to use words. She looked me straight in the eyes and began to suck the phallic barrel of the glass gun.

First, she sucked the tip, twirling her tongue around the sides. Then she swallowed it more and more deeply until she began making a soft gagging sound. Slowly, she let the saliva she'd built up drip out of her mouth and onto my cock and balls.

"This is going to feel so good," she moaned. "We need to make love to that sweet ass."

With the slightest of pressure, she worked the tip of the barrel into my wet hole. It was wild and bacchanalian, to say the least, but I trusted her. I knew the gun wasn't loaded. And even if it were, I knew she would never fire it.

Her sweet intention was the exact opposite of what I'd experienced that terrible night with the dean and the provost. And perhaps that was the brilliance of her choosing to use a gun. What better way to show me I was not a victim, I was not defined by my past.

Inch by inch, she continued tenderly working the barrel inside of me. I felt so enraptured, so cared for, my senses were entirely overtaken. I might as well have become my cock.

With steady determination, she pushed the gun inside me all the way to the trigger guard. Slowly, she pulled it out and slid it back in. Then she pulled it out and slid it in again, deeper and faster. As she did, she told me how much she loved me.

That was when I lost control. At the cellular level, I completely lost control. There was no "I" left to control.

There was just the pleasure, the wonder, the mystery of our intersecting souls. I came and I came and I came. And I came some more.

When at last I was fully spent, everything merged into oneness—absolutely everything. The universe was simply one. One and one and one.

And the one was love.

And the love was one.

THIRTY-FIVE

Possibly Number Two

When I woke up, it was almost noon and the sun was streaming into the east-facing window of the eleventh bedroom. Our naked, spooning bodies laid on top of the bed, not under any covers. The first thing I saw was a perfect shadow of the two of us cast by the light onto a hand-carved Moroccan armoire.

I wasn't sure whether I was happy or sad to have confirmation that the Tuscan villa did indeed exist. It was beautiful, it was gorgeous, and it had unquestionably facilitated the most profound experience of my life. But to own such a thing —that was not me in the least. And there was no way that my off-hand comment about the algorithm warranted such a pay-off.

Alex understood my concerns completely. She smothered me with kisses and insisted she didn't care about status or material things. She was willing to spend the rest of our days in the Travato, she assured me.

I told her how much her words meant and, more importantly, how much our evening together had healed me. Without a doubt, I was not the same man I had been. I'd been reborn into someone who was genuinely free thanks to her courage and bravery and love.

She said that whatever freedom I'd found was wholly my own doing, but that she too felt the same. We were unconstrained souls now. Houses or cars or other trappings of wealth were irrelevant.

By way of saying goodbye to the wonderful villa, Il Castello dell'Anima, she made us a breakfast of avocado and kale toast. We consumed it on a veranda framed by trumpet flowers and overlooking Escondido beach. Alex's only request was to be allowed to indulge in the Olympic-sized pool as she'd been a competitive swimmer in high school and college.

I agreed without reservation, especially since she ripped off all of her clothes as she leaped into the pool. After admiring her bodily form for a few laps, I decided to head over to John's estate. It seemed prudent to clear things up with him before any misunderstandings escalated.

I FOUND John sitting in the lotus position next to a sunflower garden. As soon as he saw me, he gave me a huge smile with puppy dog eyes. I felt a twinge of guilt over my plan to return the villa to him, but I knew our friendship would mean nothing if I couldn't show my true self.

"Paul," he said gleefully, "how'd you enjoy those gummies?"

"Somehow I doubt you need to ask," I laughed. "What the hell was in those things?" I had to admit, it was pretty classy of him to inquire about the psychedelic candy rather than his fifty million dollar transfer of real estate.

"I hope you won't take offense," he replied. "They're based on years of careful experimentation—for very special situations only. I use the cannabis blend as a base, but then I add a touch of mescaline, psilocybin, and my secret ingredient, ibogaine."

"Ibogaine? Never heard of it." My brain momentarily considered being angry about the fact that he'd also used mescaline and psilocybin in the awful incident with Deliah, but my negative emotions couldn't seem to stick.

"Ibogaine comes from the root bark of the Iboga shrub," he explained. "Historically, it was used by forest-dwelling peoples of West Africa to promote radical spiritual growth."

"It sure seemed to do a number on me."

"Did you notice being able to confront things you normally resist?"

"I did, yes."

"That's Mr. Ibogaine at work."

"Speaking of confronting things, there's something I need to tell you, John. The villa is absolutely amazing. It's an off-the-charts gesture of kindness, but I just can't accept it. It's too much. Way, way too much."

"Too much? You haven't even seen the numbers."

"The numbers?" I asked.

"The gains in profit because of your idea. Painsluts.com has gone from making two and half a day to six and a half."

"Six and a half what?"

"Million," he said matter-of-factly. "You're making me an extra four million dollars a day—that'll cover the cost of the villa in less than two weeks. Plus I've got a dozen other tube sites with even more traffic if you're okay with licensing your idea for them too."

"How can that be possible?"

"It's called capitalism, my friend. People are hungry and they've got money to burn. Massive amounts of it. You discovered a brilliant way to feed that hunger and you deserve to be fairly compensated for it."

"I don't mean to sound naive, but I've been a wage earner my whole life. I don't really grasp stuff at this kind of level."

"What if I told you that my websites are chicken feed relative to the whole operation? They're just a tiny side gig. Would that make you feel more comfortable?"

"What operation are you referring to exactly?"

"The dispensaries and the crypto exchanges—my core businesses. They generate a hundred times more than the sites do. Actually, in the case of the crypto, it's more like a thousand times."

"I'm still not exactly sure what that means."

"Let me put it to you this way. You know how Forbes tracks the richest people in the world."

"I suppose, yeah. Bezos and Gates and Musk and guys like that."

"Exactly, only the list is bullshit."

"Why is that?"

"Because they can't track wealth held in shell companies, trusts, and offshore accounts, which is where all my serious money sits."

"Interesting."

"So my buddy Elon isn't really number three—and he'd have no problem with me telling you that."

"Not sure what you're driving at, but okay."

"What I'm saying is you're looking at number three."

My jaw dropped as the significance of his comment began to penetrate my skull.

"Or possibly number two," he added, "depending on how bitcoin is trading this morning."

"Holy fucking crap. I had no idea. So you're saying I shouldn't feel guilty taking such a big payout because you're totally loaded?"

"No, I'm not saying that at all. I only want you to do whatever's right for you. I'm not trying to impress you or influence you or push you where you don't want to go. Not in the least. I just want you to know that I support you in following any dream you have. Any dream at all. You totally deserve it, you've earned it, and I stand behind you. I stand behind the real you one hundred percent. I'm your brother, Paul. I love and accept you. Completely."

My eyes started to moisten because I never thought I'd hear words like that being said to me, especially not so honestly and with such heartfelt conviction. Nobody had ever spoken to me that way in my entire life. And the truth was, I'd given up hope on ever hearing any words of that sort. I'd given up hope a long, long, long time ago.

He put his arms around me and we held each other next to the sunflower garden for several minutes. As we did, the sunflowers turned in John's direction. Slowly, they all adjusted their orientation toward him as if he were an actor in a play and they were the audience.

Maybe they felt the light coming from within John even more than they felt the light from the sun. I didn't really know. But I remember thinking how funny it was that we were standing in the garden of a fifty million dollar estate and I was hugging a man who was worth close to a trillion dollars and the sunflowers couldn't care less about his wealth, just his light.

And I felt exactly the same way.

THIRTY-SIX

Turnabout is Fair Play

AFTER JOHN STOPPED HUGGING ME, we stood still and gazed into each other's eyes. We continued for a surprisingly long time—what some people might say was too long. I hadn't held another person's gaze so intently since the staring contests of my youth.

I could have kept going for a lot longer, not because there was anything romantic between us, but because he really did feel like a brother. He felt like the brother I lost when my parents got divorced. I'm pretty sure John considered me the same way, but we didn't get a chance to talk about it because Seth, one of his associates, came racing up to us with news.

"We have all forty-three," he said excitedly.

"With confirmed locations?" asked John.

"Affirmative. Tracked and confirmed."

"Good work, Seth. What's the dispersal look like?"

"They're all in the U.S., mostly on the west coast. But get this."

"What?"

"Every single one of them is a relative of Walter's. Mostly first and second cousins, but a few uncles too."

"Woah," I interjected.

"What's the angle?" said John.

"They all trace back to the Swedish slave traders in Walter's ancestry. Seems that's the glue that binds this group. That's why they're so obsessed with repeat offenses. When a victim lives in perpetual fear of being raped again, it's the closest thing to enslaving them, at least in the minds of these sickos."

"So they're trying to relive their ancestors' experiences?" I ventured.

"Yeah, something like that. To the best of their abilities anyway. From what we've pieced together, they seem to believe they're carrying on their legacy this way."

"That's the most disgusting thing I've ever heard in my life," I said.

"It's up there," agreed Seth. "Their factory was one of the biggest suppliers of iron chains used in the slave trade. Worldwide."

"So what are we going to do about it?" I asked in a panicked voice. "Something has to be done to stop them. The victims need help immediately."

"Without a shadow of a doubt," replied John. "We're going to stop them. You have my word on that."

"But how? How exactly? I need to be involved."

He put his hand on my shoulder. "Of course, Paul. You're the leader of this whole thing. You know that, right?"

I nodded my head in agreement, although I didn't feel like much of a leader.

"Come on," he said. "Let's give you a quick tour of the tactical area."

The three of us walked down a path to what looked to be a guest house. Its exterior featured the same Mediterranean style as the main house, but when we went inside, I saw that the walls had been gutted to create a large command center. The room was filled with computer equipment and about thirty people were seated at workstations. All of them faced a giant screen on the rear wall that displayed the real-time locations of the forty-three rapists, as well as the five hundred and thirty-four victims.

After I'd had a chance to absorb the lay of the land, John introduced me to his colleagues. Their qualifications and breadth of experience were truly staggering. He'd assembled a team of intelligence analysts, covert ops specialists, military strategists, game theorists, security experts, and computer hackers rivaling that of many first-world nations.

The team members were in the midst of debating various options for how to shut down the rapists. One of the experts displayed a Powerpoint presentation weighing the pros and cons of their top ten approaches. Most of the strategies involved commando-like raids using paid mercenaries.

A recurring question was whether to involve law enforcement and, if so, in what capacity. The overwhelming consensus was to keep the operation in-house for as long as possible, but some of the experts favored handing over the rapists once they'd been detained and made full confessions. Others took a more hard-line stance.

After running through a labyrinth of complex considerations, they turned to me for my opinion on the matter. "What do you think?" asked Seth. "Any words of wisdom?"

"I'm not sure I can offer much in that department," I said humbly. "But I want you all to know how grateful I am. It's obvious you're doing phenomenal work. I'm still in a state of shock that you've managed to track down the rapists so quickly. That's a really big deal to me, so thank you. Thank you all."

The experts nodded politely amongst themselves.

"But what option do you like best?" called out Seth. "You must have an opinion."

"The truth is, I'm not so sure I like any of them," I said, surprised by my own boldness. "I tend to be a bit of a contrarian. All the strategies you have on the table are sensible and well thought out, I'll grant you that. But they're also predictable, they follow the conventional wisdom, and I just don't think that's going to fly with this group. If we want to catch these bastards off-guard, we need an approach that lies completely outside of the box—something they wouldn't anticipate in a million years."

"Do you have anything specific in mind?" he replied.

"I'm... I'm not exactly sure," I stuttered, trying to find my words. And then my eyes caught John's and a wild idea came rushing to me. "How about we take advantage of our host's considerable expertise in the psychedelic arena?"

"The psychedelic arena?" Seth looked at me like I was a stark-raving lunatic.

"Yes, I have a feeling that a visit from Mr. Ibogaine could be the golden ticket we seek."

"Mr. Ibogaine?" he repeated. "Is he on our consultancy list?"

"I'm not seeing that name anywhere in our contacts," said another team member.

"Is anyone else here familiar with a Mr. Ibogaine?" said a third member.

"Indeed, I am," John replied. "And I believe Paul's suggestion is a brilliant one. Spectacularly brilliant. In fact, I only wish I'd thought of it myself."

"Please enlighten us," said Seth. "What exactly does this person bring to the table?"

John turned to face the other team members with a twinkle in his eyes. "Have any of you ever heard of the expression, 'turnabout is fair play?' I think that may be the best way to understand what Mr. Ibogaine can do for us in this situation."

THIRTY-SEVEN

If You Put It Like That

WHEN THE OTHER team members learned about Mr. Ibogaine, they mostly resisted the idea of employing his assistance for our operation. But I spoke passionately about how much he'd helped me—in the form of John's fabled rainbow gummies. And I emphasized that ibogaine was just one small part of my proposed strategy.

The heart of the plan involved daring to speak the absolute unvarnished truth. In my experience, the most blunt, direct, and throw-caution-to-the-wind version of the truth seemed to have more capacity to effect change than just about anything else. Finding the fortitude to speak that brand of truth wasn't always easy, but it was what made my approach outside of the box.

John got the concept right away. I barely needed to explain the mechanics to him and he did a great job of fleshing it out for the others. For all I knew, it was his idea before it was mine and he was just clever enough to wait for me to mention it.

In any case, after much debate, and in recognition of the fact that John held the purse strings, the team members finally signed onto our wild and crazy plot. From there it was simply a matter of John placing some cold calls. The first one was to our good old buddy Walter.

"Mr. Olaffson?" he said from a secure line, to which we all listened. "You don't know me, but my name is John Laster. I'm an obscenely rich man and I also happen to be a close friend of your ex-son-in-law, Paul."

"Yes?" Walter replied tentatively. "What can I do for you?"

"I know about the rapes, all of them, and I want to help you stop committing them."

"Excuse me? Is this some kind of prank?"

"It is most indeed not a prank. I'm prepared to give you fifty million dollars just for coming over to my house in Malibu this Saturday at 1 pm. Paul will be there too. And if you listen to me talk and follow my instructions, I'll give you another nine hundred and fifty million dollars a couple of hours later. By the end of the afternoon, you'll have a billion dollars to do whatever you want with."

"And the GT R," I called out in the background.

"This is bullshit," said Walter. "Fuck you." And he hung up.

John proceeded to call the other forty-two rapists and make the same offer. The majority of them also hung up on him. Not a single one agreed to his proposal.

Later in the week, they received formal invitations to the event, along with detailed instructions for how to claim the initial fifty million in the form of bitcoin. And—surprise, surprise—by Friday evening, all forty-three rapists had successfully transferred the payments into their crypto wallets.

The rapists weren't stupid, of course. They did their due diligence. They confirmed Laster's capital accumulations and verified his absence of contact with law enforcement. And many of them swiftly cashed out their bitcoin wallets in favor of U.S. dollars.

The only thing that really mattered, however, was that all forty-three of them showed up at Laster's estate at 1 pm on that fateful Saturday. They came in Teslas, Hummers, helicopters, Harleys, and even armored vehicles. But came they did.

Walter arrived with Iolana by her side and I rushed out to greet them both. "Welcome to Point Dume," I enthused. "The roadster is now yours, as promised." I shook Walter's befuddled hand and slipped him the key to the GT R.

"I'm disappointed to see you're mixed up in this nonsense, son," he replied. "Very disappointed."

Alex overheard his comment and came up to him. "Hopefully," she said, "after you hear what John has to say, you won't still feel that way."

He just pursed his lips and continued walking to the lounge, where the visitors were being ushered. Iolana stayed behind to give Alex a long embrace and I followed up with a kiss on her cheek. As I did, she whispered in my ear, "I believe in both of you. And I believe in John too."

"Thank you, mom," I said.

It was the first time I'd ever called her that. I stared into her eyes, into the eyes of my true mother, long enough to be sure that she felt likewise. Then we all proceeded to the lounge.

I joined John, Bunni, and Alex on a makeshift platform, while the rapists found seats on plush yoga mats arranged in front of the stage. The wives, girlfriends, and significant others occupied chairs in the rear of the lounge.

"Hello there," said John, once everyone had arrived. "I'm so glad you could make it. I'm sure you have many questions and I'll happily answer them, but first we have a little business to tend to. For those of you seeking the nine hundred and fifty million dollar bonus payment, I need you to pop one of these rainbow gummies in your mouth. They're completely safe, I've eaten hundreds of them, and they contain the highest quality blend of cannabis, mescaline, psilocybin, and ibogaine in a very special ratio that I developed myself."

He held up one of the gummies for everyone to see and placed it into his own mouth. Meanwhile, a team of workers wearing purple polo shirts began distributing them to the forty-three rapists. Not surprisingly, they appeared unenthusiastic.

"You can swallow them, chew them or suck them," he continued, "but you must do so in the presence of one of our attendants wearing a purple shirt. Once they confirm that you've fully ingested your gummy, you'll be good to go. After that, all you'll need to do is stick around and listen to what we have to say. In a couple of hours, the bonus payment will be transferred to your wallets."

"What if we refuse?" a guest called out.

"No problem," said John. "Participation is entirely optional. You can leave whenever you want and still keep your fifty million. Just be aware that if you choose not to ingest your gummy or if you miss any part of our presentation, then you cannot collect the additional nine hundred and fifty million."

"And what if this drug of yours causes a bad reaction?" asked another guest.

"We have trained nurses on staff to assist with any adverse side effects, but such things are very rare, I assure you."

"You expect us to just take your word for it? That's nuts!"

"I understand your concern. In an ideal world, we'd have more time to establish trust, but this is an exceptional situation and that's why such a large amount of money is in play. We all have different risk/reward curves. Only you know if it's worthwhile. If nine hundred and fifty million dollars is not a big enough incentive to undergo the risk, that's entirely your call."

"Why so much money? What's in it for you?"

"Great question," he replied. "Let me tell you exactly."

"Damn straight, you'd better tell us," cried out another guest. "Else we can't vouch for your safety!"

"Safety, yes, safety," John said slowly. "I don't know about you, but I myself did not enjoy a safe childhood. I was raised in the Mojave desert in a four by six-foot shed where I was kept hog-tied in my own feces, in pitch dark, for the better part of every day. My father raped me in that shed over two thousand times—until I finally escaped at age fourteen. My mother raped me two hundred and thirteen times. I have the exact count for my mother because she didn't begin raping me until age eleven and by then I had taught myself basic arithmetic. My father started on me much earlier, so that accounts for the inexact estimate. I had two brothers and two sisters who lived in sheds like mine, and my parents raped them with similar frequency until my older brother Jack tried to fight back. That didn't go so well for him and my father ended up killing him when he was twelve. My other brother and my two sisters committed suicide before their sixteenth birthdays." He paused to study the guests.

"So I guess you could say I have skin in this game," he continued. "I might not descend from slave traders, but I do know a bit about being on the other side of captivity. That's what's in it for me. Would you say that's a fair assessment, Bunni?"

"Yes, dear," she replied. "That's a very fair assessment. Understated, if anything, is all I would add."

"Thank you, sweetheart. I appreciate that. Bunni is my dear, devoted girlfriend who singlehandedly saved my life. Why don't you tell our guests a bit about what's in it for you?"

"Of course," said Bunni. "At the age of four, I was kidnapped by an international sex-trafficking outfit. For the next two decades, they whored me out to whoever would pay the most—sheiks, oil barons, CEOs, terrorists, politicians, arms dealers, you name it. Every orifice of my body was regularly invaded, day in and day out, and I received a steady stream of beating, torture, and humiliation as an accompaniment. I didn't keep count, but I was raped at least three to four times a day, minimum. I think that adds up to over twenty thousand rapes, right, dear?"

"Yes, I believe it does," said John. "I believe that qualifies you with skin in the game."

"Thanks, honey."

"And that brings us to Alex," he continued. "Would you

like to say a little something to help our guests with the orientation?"

She stood up and approached the audience. "Yes, I would. Thank you, John. My name is Alex and, at the age of eight, I was raped by my best friend's father. It happened on just one occasion, although he raped me multiple times, so my story might sound inconsequential compared to John's or Bunni's. But I lost my best friend because of it—not to mention my self-worth and my trust in humanity. And the pedophile who raped me is sitting here today among you, so maybe that qualifies me too." She smiled benignly at the audience.

"Thank you, Alex," said John. "I'd say you're supremely qualified. And Paul? Do you have anything you'd like to add?"

I walked up beside Alex and held her hand. "Yes, I do. This same man who raped Alex went on to rape his own daughter a few years later. Before that, he raped her mother —that's how the daughter was brought into this world. So he raped the mom, the daughter, and her best friend and then he raped dozens more, thanks to the system you guys set up on Signal."

The rapists began to fidget in their seats and a few of them let out muffled boos.

"Oh," I continued, "and that daughter ended up becoming my wife. She married me because she could tell I was a victim too—I was raped by my father's colleagues at age eight. Unfortunately, she was so traumatized by every-thing she'd suffered that she couldn't remain married to me. She committed suicide right here in Malibu just a few weeks ago. That's how I ended up meeting Paul and Bunni and

Alex." I stared straight into Walter's eyes as I spoke this last sentence.

"Now you know why John asked you all to come here," said Alex. "That's what's in it for us. Does that make any sense?"

The guests looked even more dumbstruck than before. Their defenses seemed to have slightly faded—at least enough to look more closely at the gummies they held in their hands. But they took no action and said nothing.

"I don't know what the hell more you need from us," blurted Bunni. "If you want my honest opinion, none of you are worth even close to nine hundred and fifty million dollars."

"Bunni, we talked about this," replied John. "Let's let them reach their own conclusions without judgment." He turned to the guests. "Please forgive her. This is not easy."

Kindness and good intention emanated from his face in such a genuine way that it was undeniable. Everyone could see that he expected nothing from the rapists, that he doubted they would ingest his gummies, and that he accepted the madness of humanity exactly as it was. Like a wizened bodhisattva, he held no agenda whatsoever.

"So," said Bunni, "are you going to do what John asked, or are you not? I've got much better ways to spend my time than hanging out here with you creeps, so if you don't want to take him up on his offer, then I'd appreciate it if you'd get the hell out of here. Now."

"Oh, geez," said one guest.

"Well, if you put it like that," said another.

"Fuck it," said a third.

And then, one by one, every single rapist inserted a gummy in his mouth.

And so did Bunni.

And so did Alex.

And so did I.

THIRTY-EIGHT

Casting Long Shadows

WHILE WAITING for the gummies to take effect, John spoke of evolution and his hopes for the future. He emphasized to his guests that the human species was at a critical tipping point. Either we would cease our divisive behaviors and ensure the safety of all or we would self-destruct under the weight of our accumulated traumas.

He explained that rape was an ancient response to an unjust, unfulfilling world. Blaming, punishing, imprisoning, or rehabilitating would never put an end to it, as long as there remained unmet needs. In his view, the only solution was universal loving-kindness. If everyone would adopt this practice immediately, all of our problems would be solved.

Initially, the rapists rolled their eyes at John's idealism. What did his blathering have to do with each of their unique situations—their sufferings, their betrayals, their sorrows, and agonies? Why should *they* have to change when there were untold multitudes engaging in just as atrocious behaviors, if not worse?

But as John's mixture of cannabis, mescaline, psilocybin, and ibogaine wound its way into their bloodstreams, they found his words increasingly melodious. Their rigidities and defenses softened, their perceptual apparatuses expanded, and their habitual attachments faded. A crevice of opportunity opened in their tight skulls.

Yes, it was true. They were indeed wounded souls. Yes, it was true. They were perpetuating a cycle of abuse spanning many generations. Yes, it was true. Their aggressions were causing their own suffering, as well as that of others.

While John expounded upon his vision for humanity, another prodding voice murmured in the back of their minds as well: "One billion dollars, one billion dollars, one billion dollars." The transformative possibilities of this potential bounty lubricated the rapists' synapses and increased their receptivity.

Sensing the opportunity, John announced it was time for sacred ceremony. In the background, "Eternal Om" began to play over the speakers. He initiated a round of deep breathing, then engaged in a lengthy gratitude chant.

By the time he completed his tribute to the seven directions, the forty-three rapists were like well-trained pups, eager to please and perform. He asked them to lie down on their backs for the body scan meditation and they did so without protest. He instructed them to search their bodies for points of tension and they began sweeping them away with their proprioceptors.

Within a matter of minutes, they were cleared of stressors and wide open to the universe. In their psychedelic, Buddha-like state, they could at last see clearly, free from the myriad biases that once deluded them. Their world had become warm and cuddly, safe and non-threatening.

With the stage set, John proceeded to call in the first of the victims. Unbeknownst to the rapists, all five hundred and thirty-four of them were assembled on his estate. They were waiting patiently, sipping boba tea in a grassy meadow just a few hundred feet from the lounge.

For each rapist, one matching victim was brought into the lounge to stand before his or her subjugator. The victims held out their hands to shake while the purple-clad attendants wafted sage smoke. Mr. Ibogaine arrived on the scene with them, as if on cue.

"I'm sorry," wailed the rapists, one after another, like dominoes falling. "I apologize. I apologize. I'm very, very sorry."

The victims said nothing in reply. They'd been coached to remain perfectly silent. Instead, with merciful faces, they motioned for the rapists to get on all fours. The attendants assisted with the positioning, then they handed each of the victims a phallus-shaped gun fashioned from the pink-colored glass.

The guns were Bunni's idea. Alex had shown her the one from the Kali sculpture and it had so captured her fancy that she'd immediately set out to have copies made. What iconic symbol could possibly be more transformative, especially under the guidance of Mr. Ibogaine?

The attendants calmly suggested that the rapists remove their pants. They complied without self-consciousness, as they were no longer subject to societal norms. Like pilgrims seeking redemption, they dropped their briefs too, exposing their buttocks for all to see. A few gasps issued from the spectators in the chairs, but in their sober state, they recognized they were witnessing history.

The victims proceeded to lubricate the barrels of their guns with coconut oil. Slowly and methodically, they rubbed the tips against the rapists' smooth white butt cheeks. Teasing and titillating their oppressors' posteriors, while periodically grazing their testicles and perineal regions, they waited for a sign from John.

When the gummies reached their maximum efficacy, he subtly nodded his head. The victims knew to commence their task in earnest. With steady but determined pressure, they inserted the phallic barrels into the rapists' sphincters.

"Yeeeeeh ooooooh aaaaaaah!" moaned the rapists in agony and ecstasy.

The victims paid no attention and continued inserting the guns.

"Do you want more?" asked John. "Do you need more?"

"Yes! No! Yes!" they begged. "Please stop! Please don't stop!"

The victims pushed the phallic guns still deeper inside the rapists' anal cavities before slightly retracting them. After a brief moment, they thrust them in once more, this time all the way. Then with no forewarning—bang!—they pulled the triggers in synchrony.

The rapists collapsed to the ground, sobbing and crying and blubbering. They assumed, quite reasonably, that bullets had been lodged deep inside their colons. They assumed they were dying, that blood was seeping from their internal organs.

"We deserve it!" they yowled, as directed by Mr. Ibogaine. "We need it! This is fair! Thank you!"

In fact, however, the guns had been outfitted with electronic cartridges that produced the sound of a gunshot, but contained no primer or gunpowder. The rapists had not been injured, at least not physically. Still, there was more learning to be done.

John nodded his head again. Stoically, the second round of victims entered the lounge. They traded places with the first group and withdrew the guns from the rapists' rectums.

"Time to shake hands," said John.

The rapists picked themselves up from the ground and struggled to regain their composure. They were relieved to still be alive but surprised that the ceremony had not yet ended. As the attendants wafted more sage smoke, the victims held out their hands to shake.

"I'm sorry," they cried again. "I apologize. I apologize. I'm very, very sorry."

As before, this round of victims said nothing in reply, instead motioning for the rapists to get on all fours. They rubbed the tips of the guns against the rapists' butt cheeks, teased their testicles and perineums, then reinserted the phallic barrels into their sphincters.

"Yeeeeeh ooooooh aaaaaaah!"

"Do you want more, do you need more?" asked John.

"Yes! No! Yes!"

The victims pushed the barrels in and out of their anal cavities, then thrust them to the hilt. They pulled the triggers in unison. Bang!

"We deserve it! We need it! This is fair! Thank you!"

And so the cycle repeated itself until all five hundred and thirty-four victims had faced their tormentors, lodged the gun barrels deep inside their assholes, and pulled the triggers. Each rapist experienced ten to fifteen such cycles, depending on the number of rapes committed. By then, they'd had more than enough opportunity to confront their misdeeds.

Of course, were it not for Mr. Ibogaine and the magic of the rainbow gummies, the rapists would have had a wall of defenses in place. They would not have so easily overcome their knee-jerk denials and rationalizations. But as it stood, all of the rapists reached the same conclusion with uniformity.

"Our ancestors were wrong!"

"We were wrong!"

"Rape is a crime against humanity!

"Slavery is a crime against humanity!"

"We beg forgiveness!"

"Never again! Never ever again!"

John gave his nod and the victims withdrew the guns from the rapists' rectums for the final time. They set the guns on the ground beside the yoga mats. Then they quietly filed out of the lounge and returned to the grassy meadow.

"We've now come to the end of our session," said John, glancing at his watch. "As promised, it's been less than two hours since you arrived. You may put your pants back on and collect your bonus payments. You've all qualified for the nine hundred and fifty million."

"We're not worthy!" shouted one of the rapists.

"We don't deserve it!" cried another.

"Give it to the victims instead!" yelled a third.

"Is that how you all feel?" asked John.

"Yes! Yes! Yes!" they agreed.

"You're a hundred percent sure?"

"Yes! Yes! Yes!"

"Would you like to divide the proceeds equally among all the victims?"

"Yes! Yes! Yes!"

John pulled out his phone and made some quick calculations. "In that case," he said, "each victim will get a little over seventy-six million dollars."

"That's not enough!"

"We want to return the fifty million you gave each of us too!"

"Give it to the victims instead!"

"You're sure about that?" asked John.

"Yes! Yes! Yes!"

"Very well," he replied. "That means each victim will get eighty million dollars. Does that sound better?"

"Yes! Yes! Yes!"

The rapists picked up their phones and opened their crypto wallets. Those who hadn't cashed out the initial payment transferred it back to John. Those that had cashed out took the necessary steps to undo their transfers. Meanwhile, the attendants helped the victims set up their own crypto wallets, where needed.

John then divided the forty-three billion dollars he'd allocated for the rapists and distributed it equally to the five hundred and thirty-four victims. It took about an hour to complete all the transactions, but compared with how difficult a settlement would have been through the courts, the procedure was startlingly easy.

I'd asked Gene Maher to attend the event in case we ran into legal questions, so John checked with him to see if we needed to memorialize the transfers in writing or take any other protective actions. He assured us it wasn't necessary. The transfers were gifts, pure and simple.

Gene explained that the victims could still pursue lawsuits against the rapists if they so wished. Since the payments were coming directly from John, they had no bearing on any remedies the victims might be eligible to receive. None of them seemed interested in pursuing legal action, but it put my mind at ease to know they weren't giving up any options.

I felt bad for Bunni and Alex and Iolana, however, as they weren't part of the five hundred and thirty-four, yet they'd been victims too. When I mentioned my concern to John, he gave me one of his long gazes before replying.

"You make an excellent point, Paul," he said. "I'm an absolute idiot for not thinking about that."

"It's okay," I replied. "You've had a lot on your mind and this is tricky stuff."

"Fortunately, there's an easy solution—at least insofar as money can address the horrors to which they've been subjected." And he proceeded to transfer eighty million dollars to each of them too.

There were sobs and tears and even some hugs, as the guests began gathering their belongings and taking leave. Seeing the victims and rapists streaming out of John's estate in relative peace and harmony was probably the most surreal experience of my life. We'd done something pretty significant—or, I should say, Deliah had done something pretty significant—and it felt good to be bringing the long process to its final closure.

Of course, I realized, as did everyone else, that we'd barely scratched the surface when it came to the real underlying problem. And clearly, the vast majority of rape victims on this planet had received no justice whatsoever—nor was a wad of cash true justice anyway. Still, I took some small comfort when Walter came up to me.

"Son," he said, "I want you to know that you've been the best son-in-law a man could ever hope for, even though I've been the worst father-in-law, not to mention the worst father and the worst husband. But I hope you'll be pleased to know, I'm going to set Yo-Yo free. I've been imprisoning her from the day I first met her and that ends now. Thank you, son. I will never forget you, just as I'll never forget Deliah."

He reached to shake my hand and as he did he pushed the key fob for the GT R into my palm. Then he walked off, with the sun setting behind him, casting long shadows onto the manicured grounds of John's estate.

Only I didn't notice the shadows and I didn't even care about them.

THIRTY-NINE

Like Tendrils from a Vine

AFTER THE GUESTS left and the attendants were paid, John, Bunni, Alex, and I walked over to the guest house. Seth popped some bottles of champagne and we celebrated with the team of experts. There were congratulatory speeches, high-fives, backslaps, and even some confetti and streamers—all reasonable responses to a job well done.

As I sipped champagne, I put my arm around Alex and tried my best to enjoy the afterglow of our success. It occurred to me that Deliah had indeed executed on the 'promise' she'd made during my first psychedelic experience. She *was* still with us. Our plan never would have succeeded had she not been.

But even so, I couldn't seem to adopt a celebratory mood. Every time I caught John's eye, I sensed he was struggling with a similar problem. We kept flashing each other looks of concern, while somehow keeping up our appearances for the rest of the crew.

Of course, both Alex and Bunni could tell something

was up. They both tried to feed us from the lavish platters of appetizers, but neither one of us had any interest. The thought of food almost made me want to vomit.

It wasn't until midnight that the celebration ended and the four of us were finally relieved of entertaining. After hugs all around, we walked arm-in-arm through the garden and headed back to the lounge. Seemingly on auto-pilot, we passed through the arched entryway at the rear and entered the third room—the room where John and Bunni had put on their first show for me.

Why exactly we were there, none of us appeared to know. We sat in a circle, cross-legged on the big satin bed, and all took in a deep breath. One breath led to another and another until it became clear we were meditating.

A good ten minutes passed before I broke the silence. "Do we all agree the job isn't finished yet or is it just me?"

"I'm with you, brother," replied John. "Very much so. But I think we might need to apprise the women."

"Of what exactly?" asked Bunni.

"I took advantage of Gene's presence to update my trusts," he explained. "You're now my sole beneficiary."

"I don't understand," she replied.

"After those payoffs this afternoon, I believe I have a net worth of about nine hundred. But I'd like to give a hundred to Alex if you're okay with that."

"Of course," she replied. "It's whatever you want. You know that."

"A hundred what?" asked Alex.

"Billion," he said. "A hundred billion dollars. I thought you might want to set up a charitable foundation for the cause."

"That's insane." Her lips trembled as she spoke. "That might be enough money to actually do something."

"It might. And I have a feeling Bunni would match that amount down the road if you guys wanted to work together."

"Of course I would," she said. "More than match it. There's nothing else I'd want to do."

"Excellent," he replied. "I'll make the transfer." And he proceeded to send a hundred billion dollars to Alex's bitcoin wallet.

"But I still don't understand," said Bunni. "Why are we talking about this now?"

"I can't speak for John," I answered, "but I believe it boils down to how we can have the greatest impact for good going forward. I thought I'd feel a sense of completion after turning these forty-three rapists around, but the truth is, I don't."

"I don't either," said John. "You are speaking for me, brother. And this is the clearest I've ever seen you, by the way."

"What Deliah did to get us all on board was incredible," I continued. "But now we have to forge new territory. Even if it's scary, even if it's terrifying, we have to ask ourselves what would Deliah do?"

"Exactly," he replied. "I thought I was a trailblazer, but you give the term a whole new meaning. I love you, Paul Wolniak." He smoothed back my hair with his hands and kissed me softly on the forehead. "Now let's show the women some loving too."

Bunni flashed him a smile and laid back on the circular bed. He motioned for her to raise her legs and, as she did, he pulled off her skirt and panties. Then he got on his knees and began licking her genitalia.

Meanwhile, Alex beckoned me closer with her finger. She extracted the black leather dog collar from her purse—the one encrusted with gems that I'd found in the GT R after almost wiping out—and she carefully fastened it around my neck.

"Does this mean I'm yours?" I asked.

"Yes," she said. "It does."

"Forever?"

"Forever."

"And you're not mad at me?"

"How could I be?"

"It worries me that you might feel I'm choosing Deliah over you."

"Why do you think I'm putting the collar on you, silly. Besides, I love her too. And this is my choice as much as yours."

"But?"

"But it sucks to have to be strong. I don't feel like being strong." Tears began streaming down her face.

"I'm sorry," I said. "I wish you didn't have to. I really, really wish that."

"Yeah, but you've been strong as hell ever since I told you I was trans. I want to be the same for you. I believe in what you said about the greatest impact for good, so now I've got to walk the walk. Right, Master?"

I nodded my head slowly. It felt strange to be having this conversation while John and Bunni were engaged in sex a few feet away from us, but then again, everything had been strange—pretty much continuously—since the moment I first saw Deliah's Post It Note.

The only thing that made any sense whatsoever was to

flip Alex on her back, rip off her clothes, and begin fucking the shit out of her. Which is exactly what I did. And I'm pretty sure she liked it. A lot.

We went at it for a solid hour while John and Bunni did likewise. We fucked like there was no tomorrow—every hole, every position, every emotion—because, in truth, there wasn't a tomorrow for me and John, not if the rest of humanity wanted a chance. We all realized it, whether consciously or not, and the only thing good about it was that we sure as hell didn't hold back.

Right here, right now—that was all we had. Inhibitions were bullshit. Fears were bullshit. Insecurities were bullshit. Our past traumas were bullshit. Fuck them. Fuck them hard.

It was all or nothing, pedal to the metal, take it to the limit, stare straight into her eyes, reveal everything, risk everything, hold nothing back. Just raw motherfucking love. All the way down the line. To the finish.

Because I loved her that much. And she loved me that much. I knew it was the same with John and Bunni too—they were the ones who'd showed me what it was all about in the first place.

And then, when all four of us came harder than we ever had, together in unison, and we were heaped together in a pile of cum and sweat and our hearts were beating a mile a minute, John leaned towards me and looked at me so deeply that the use of words seemed laughable.

"So what do you say, brother? Is now the time?"

"Yes, brother. Now. Is. The. Time."

He reached into a cabinet drawer and pulled out two of the phallus-shaped guns fashioned from the pink-colored glass. The regular ones. He handed one to Bunni and the other to Alex.

Getting on all fours, he studied the three of us. He gazed at us with such stillness that, once again, I thought he was having some sort of seizure—until I reminded myself why.

I took my position beside him on the bed while Bunni and Alex sucked and licked the barrels of the guns. And to their credit, they even giggled. That's how fucking amazing they both were.

Then they inserted the barrels into our assholes. And yeah, they went slow and they made it feel good for us. Of course, they did. In and out, just a little at first, then more and more, until gradually they were able to work the whole barrels inside of us.

But that was as far as they could go, which made complete sense, and not just from the legal perspective. From every perspective, even from the perspective of the shadows the barrels cast onto the carpet. Even from the perspective of the shadows inside our alimentary canals.

When Bunni and Alex retreated, John and I had no choice but to reach back behind ourselves to see if we could continue the task on our own. It was almost funny because the angle just wasn't feasible. At least not for either of us.

Side by side on all fours, with the pink-colored phallus-shaped guns deep in our assholes, our hands grazed each other. They grazed each other ever so gently, as we struggled to finish the task. Like tendrils from a vine reaching to climb toward the sky, they found each other and instinctively clasped together.

We held our hands clasped together like that for even longer than one of John's famous gazes. Alex and Bunni watched the whole escapade with love oozing off their faces. And then, at the same exact moment, I reached for the gun in John's ass and John reached for the gun in mine.

And we squeezed, so be it, we squeezed.

For Deliah.

PsycheDeliah.